Ophelia in the Un

and Other Melancholy Tales

Stephen Howard

abuddhapress@yahoo.com

Stephen Howard 2023

®™©

Alien Buddha Press 2023

ISBN: 9798861109116

The following stories are works of fiction. Any similarities to actual people, places, or events, unless deliberately expressed otherwise by the author are purely coincidental.

Table of Contents

For Rachel, my wife, my muse and inspo

The Thomson Curse

I drop my case of beers on my great-grandfather's headstone, leaning my shovel beside it, and get to loading my 12-gauge shotgun. It's a newer Winchester semi-automatic. When your target moves as fast as a turkey at most, it does the job just fine.

It's a cold day. It always is, April 1st, the start of the cruellest month. The only good thing about having to come here every damn year is not getting sucked into pranks or juvenile delinquency. But this year is different. I nearly didn't come.

The house sits high on the hill, looming over the whole area, staring down at this spot. Its windows are blackened eyes, set deep within gabled eye sockets. Of course, I haven't lived in it for a long time. No one has; not since father passed. It's a house that expects a lot of us Thomsons. Some would argue it expects too much.

I crack open a beer and take a swig. Not long now. I hear a squawk and look up to see birds line the branches of the ash trees. Others perch upon the metal railings that surround our family plot. Every year, without fail, they sit patiently waiting. Like they know what's going to happen. A deep, dark secret passed down through families of birds. Keep an eye on this spot. One day, young scavengers, you will hit upon the motherload.

Earthy scents invade my nostrils. And then rotten eggs.

It's starting.

Dull groans surround me. I raise my shotgun, ready to fire. A hand bursts from beneath the matted soil. Earthworms bubble upwards like champagne for the dead. I march toward the disturbed grave and wait. Scrambling forth, one hand becomes two, followed by a desiccated head and shoulders.

"Hey gramps, good to see you." I pull the trigger and blast his skull into pieces, splattering mulched brain and skull scraps that'll sink into the earth like Miracle-Gro.

Another fist punches through its natural prison only to be met with a bullet. Someone I never knew, a great uncle, I think. Soon, a third. The investment in the Winchester is really paying off, the recoil of the semi-automatic is much lower impact than the rusty old piece of junk I'd been using up to last year. I was bruised for days after, normally.

I hear a cry, higher pitched than the usual moans and groans, and whirl round, eye down the barrel of my weapon. Ready to take out the next undead Thomson looking to wreak havoc on the unsuspecting world of the living. The cawing of crows and squawking of vultures stops. My breathing, ironically, stops.

"April," I whisper.

I cannot tear my eyes from the small, delicate hands scratching away at the soil. The 12-gauge trembles in my hands. Down the barrel, I see a mess of blonde pigtails emerge. Cute, puffy little cheeks. Button nose. But the eyes are milky and senseless and contain no recognition.

I start forward until I'm a few yards away, watching as my daughter struggles out from her early grave. Groans play upon the air around me, and birdcalls scrap with them for supremacy. A grotesque serenade. April is rising from the rough hole. There isn't even a headstone, yet.

"I'm sorry, beautiful girl," I gasp, feeling tears and snot run free down my face. "It should have been me. It should have been me."

All around me bodies are shoving their way up towards the light, the dim, cold light of April, just as they do every year. The Thomson Curse. Each year the dead arise, each year the family must send them back. And now my beautiful girl. Named after this cursed month – her mother's doing. I should have seen it was an omen. If only I hadn't fallen asleep. All I have now is a scar along my hairline. That, and memories.

Bodies stumble forth around me, towards me. I am the enemy. I am dinner. Something looms in my peripheral vision: the house is looking down at me because it knows I am the last. What will happen when I am gone? Who will rebury the dead?

April lunges for me. Not in embrace, but in blind rage.

I pull the trigger, then reload.

Loomis Creek

"I'm sure you've heard of Bigfoot. Probably think you know all about him?"

A fire crackled and small orange embers drifted about it. Four young campers – two men, two women – stared at their guide. None of them spoke and for a time only the sounds of the forest could be heard. It was a chill early evening and the full moon had yet to grace the darkening sky.

"If you'll indulge an old man, I've got a scary campfire story for you all. What do you say?"

A hint of relief was followed by a few smiles and nods – one of the men said, 'yes please, that sounds spooky', before grabbing his girlfriend's knee, causing her to jump. Encouraged by the jovial response, the old forest guide continued.

"This is a true story, you know," he said, to incredulous guffaws. The guide, a man of about sixty with long, straggly grey hair and dirtied fingernails, gazed around the circle of young friends and slowly broke out into a yellowed smile. "Judge for yourselves. You'll be thinking that Bigfoot is a shy fellow, hides in mountains and thick forests, just like this one. Well, you'd be wrong. Now let me tell you about Loomis Creek."

***

Daniel Weathers was the Chief of Police in Loomis Creek, in a department of two people, and he knew he was a lucky guy. There hadn't been a murder in

11

these parts for the best part of 40 years and he didn't expect much to change on his watch. His father had been chief before him, as tends to be the way in towns like Loomis. Buried in the heart of Washington State, Loomis was small, seven hundred or so residents, and surrounded by thick and hilly woodland, forests of Douglas firs, Sitka spruces and Mountain hemlocks sprawling in all directions. The eponymous creek ran around town then south and there was one road in and out: route 7. Main Street was decked with stores, as well as the police station, and residential roads splintered off from there.

Chief Weathers stood on the porch outside the station – an old and stoic building with big windows – and watched the locals milling about. His deputy, Mike Bryant, joined him.

"Just a call, Dan. That drunk Jim Jacobs is on his way in, says it's urgent," said Mike, his voice deep and dripping in disdain. Dan laughed.

"Don't let anyone hear you calling Loomis citizens drunks, Mike," Dan said, patting the much taller Mike on the shoulder, "no matter how true it is," he muttered, smiling.

And then they heard the screech of tyres as a truck took a corner too fast. Instinct called them both to reach for their guns, basic training kicking in, before they relaxed. Jim Jacobs's truck pulled up in front of the station like he was pitting at the Indy 500.

"What the heck are you playing at, Jim?" said Dan, marching down the porch steps and straight up to Jim's red Chrysler. Its front end was banged up and dented.

Jim, eyes watery, face flushed, jumped down from the driver's side and walked straight past the chief.

"I've got to speak to you Daniel, right now, in the station. It's a matter of life and death," he yelled, attracting the maximum amount of attention as he stormed past Deputy Bryant and through the station door. Predictably, the smell of ale followed him in.

Entering the station to find Jim sat before his desk, Dan nodded at Mike, who grabbed a pen and paper.

"First of all, Jim, it's Chief Weathers. Second, have you been drinking? Third, if I see you drive your truck around Loomis like that again I'll have you in a cell. Fourth, why are you here?" said Dan, easing back in his seat. Mike pulled up a chair alongside the desk and Jim eyeballed him with suspicion. Dan knew full well what an old racist Jim Jacobs was and exactly why he was leering at the 6 foot plus black police officer watching him with indifference.

"Jim," Dan prompted.

"Oh, right. No, I ain't been drinking, not since last night. And don't give me the tough guy stuff Daniel, I remember you in diapers. But I'll go with Chief

Weathers if it means you listen to this. Christ have mercy on my soul, I do not tell lies. You saw the front of my truck? Well I was on the road late last night…"

"I thought you were drinking last night?" Mike interrupted.

"That was after, after! I was driving up the country road, driving back from my cousin's place up in Buckley, when I had to swerve off the road. Man, you ain't seen nothing like it. This thing came lumbering out the trees, must've been eight feet tall, easy. Looked like a big gorilla. I panicked and swung the wheel and crashed right into the trees back on route 7. I was lucky the bush was thick and softened the blow. I got a mighty whack to the head, see," Jim said, pointing to a fresh cut on his forehead. He had some light bruising around his eye, too.

"So you swung to avoid a deer, and crashed your truck? It's not exactly life or death, Jim, as sorry as I am to hear that," said Dan, leaning forward to inspect the cut on Jim's head. "Maybe get that looked at by a doctor though."

Jim slammed his hand down hard on the table.

"No, goddammit. Excuse my cussing, but I ain't talking about no deer. This was no animal I ever saw and it was half a mile out of town. I heard it make this loud, rumbling cry and run off. I think maybe it got spooked because another car happened on up the road and helped me get myself right. But no, they didn't see nothing. I'm telling you Daniel, there's something in the woods and it ain't natural."

***

14

"What do you think?" asked Dan, turning on the coffee machine. They'd only just convinced Jim Jacobs to leave, under threat of arrest for anything from driving under the influence to wasting police time.

"I think he's a heavy drinker with a history of driving drunk who probably banged his car into his own damn gate," said Mike, taking a cup of coffee and laughing. "That man is terrified of me. If he wasn't so pathetic it'd get to me more maybe, I don't know. But he sure as hell didn't see no giant ape out on route 7."

Dan nodded. He could hear it starting to rain outside. It had been like that the past few days, raining on and off.

Something about Jim's insistence had rattled him, but he and Mike were both young officers and this was just about the sleepiest town in America. If he went about chasing after Jim Jacobs's hallucinations the department would quickly become a laughing stock.

"Full moon again tonight," said Mike, putting his feet on his desk. "Your wife is into all that crystal stuff, right? What's she saying is gonna happen?" he laughed.

"She's not one for making predictions," Dan joked, "if I ever ask, she puts on a spooky voice and says, 'evil doers lurk in the darkness'."

***

It was 5am when Dan got the call.

By 5:20am he was on the scene, closely followed by Mike. Both of them stared wide-eyed at the body on the ground. They were by the local autoshop, which faced Main Street, right next to route 7 heading out of town. Mike turned to be sick on the grass verge, while Dan, only just gulping down vomit himself, pushed the few early-bird bystanders back and began to secure the area.

It was still dark, but the autoshop's forecourt lights illuminated the roadside. What the light revealed was the corpse of a man. In a small town like Loomis, everyone knows everyone, so Mike and Dan knew who they were looking at. But the face was so brutally disfigured, they could hardly tell. It was the mechanic's overalls and logo that told them this was Bill Hicks. Savage tears criss-crossed his body. His right arm lay several feet away.

"It's got to be an animal attack, right?" said Mike, lurching over to where Dan stood.

"Got to be," replied Dan, his eyes focused on the dismembered arm.

"No person could cause those injuries. No way."

Dan nodded and continued to stare.

"Head back to the station and call county, please Mike. We're gonna need an ME to examine the body at the least."

"Sure thing, boss," said Mike. He turned to go but stopped. "What is it?"

"Not sure," said Dan, striding up the road. The recent rains had softened the surrounding terrain. Either side of the road out of town was muddy and littered with puddles.

"Holy shit."

"What…?" said Mike, joining him. Mike put his arm on Dan's shoulder to steady himself, his legs almost collapsing beneath him.

Marked distinctly in the mud was the largest footprint either of them had ever seen.

***

Following a long discussion with the county sheriff's office, Dan, leaving Mike to wait for the medical examiner, took the cruiser to Bill Hick's home. His wife Nancy needed informing.

It was a short trip up town on which he passed the familiar red Chrysler truck of Jim Jacobs.

Dan pulled up outside the Hicks's residence. Walking up the path, he told himself he was Chief Weathers, Chief Weathers. Cold morning light needled any exposed flesh. Shaking his hands out, Dan took a deep breath and rang the doorbell.

Nancy Hicks answered the door. Her eyes were puffy and red.

"You're late," she said, walking back into the house and turning into the dining room, leaving Dan stood in the doorway.

Closing the door behind him, he followed Nancy through and took up a seat beside her. A bottle of whisky sat on the table alongside two glasses.

"Nancy, I'm very sorry but…" Dan began, before Nancy held up a hand to stop him. Before speaking, she poured a drink and sank half of it.

"My husband is dead."

Dan nodded a yes but said nothing more.

"Jim came straight here to tell me. A greater courtesy than our police chief managed. Jim told me everything," Nancy said, her eyes fixed on Dan's face, though he struggled to meet her gaze.

"I… I'm sorry, Nancy. I had to speak to the county sheriff to organise the autopsy, but then I came straight to you, I promise."

"Seems the apple has fallen quite far from the tree, wouldn't you say? Your father was a fine chief. A fine man. If a concerned citizen told him about a dangerous animal roaming near the town, he wouldn't have been so dismissive. And now my Bill…" Nancy stopped, tears flowing down her face, her breathing heavier. "My Bill has paid the price."

"Nancy, I'm really sorry about Bill, I am. I don't know how much Jim has said, but nothing he reported to the police is related to Bill's death. I'm not here to talk about Jim Jacobs, I'm here to offer you all the support I can at this time. I also need to ask you a couple of questions about Bill. Is that okay?"

Nancy blew her nose on a tissue and nodded in response.

"Does Bill usually get to his garage as early as he did today?" said Dan, pulling his notepad from his shirt pocket. He looked around at the dining room. Decorative teapots filled the shelves of a glass-cased cupboard. Family photos hung from hooks on the walls.

"He does. Every day. You should really know that, Dan. He starts early and finishes early. Stays on call for any breakdowns in the evening. Why?" Nancy asked, drying her eyes with another tissue.

"Just establishing that Bill was going about his normal day. But it looks like some sort of animal attack, Nancy. I am really sorry. I'll speak with Sally to put together a group to track and kill whatever did this to Bill," Dan said. He placed his hand on Nancy's, but she pulled away.

"Just do your job, Dan," she said, standing and looking towards the door.

***

Mike was still on the phone upon Dan's return. He eyed Dan as he entered and shook his head, made a gun shape with his hand, and pretended to blow his brains out.

Any incident saw a spike in phone calls from nosy locals. News travelled fast in Loomis.

Mike slammed the phone down.

"Jim Jacobs?" Dan asked.

"That son of a bitch has told half the town Bill Hicks was killed by an animal he warned us was nearby. You know what people are like, they're lapping it up. Jim seems to have left out the bit about an 8-foot gorilla."

"He told Nancy Hicks the same thing before I got to her. She's pissed with us. Well, pissed with me. I told her we don't believe the thing Jim is talking about is connected to Bill's death…" said Dan. Rain began to fall and pitter-patter on the station roof.

"And the footprint?" said Mike, standing and walking to the window.

"I don't know, man. What are we saying? Bigfoot walked into town and beat Bill Hicks to death?"

"Heck, what if it's true?"

"I don't want to hear it… Oh shit, is that Sandra? Christ, that's all we need," Dan said. He was itching for a cigarette. He'd quit a few months back but hadn't anticipated something this stressful would come along and tickle his lungs.

Mike opened the station door and wordlessly turned from the woman, who had perfectly coiffed hair, bright rouge lips, and wore a matching royal blue skirt and blazer, now stood in the doorway. They'd had what you might call an acrimonious break-up.

"Hey Mike, we're going to need to organise a hunting party. Can you talk to Sally Lee? Best head up to her store," Dan asked. "Sandra, take a seat," he added.

"Will do, chief," said Mike. He grabbed his bomber jacket and left.

"He really can't be in the same room as me, can he?" Sandra said, laughing bitterly. Sandra was an attractive thirtysomething with more ambition than Loomis could contain. Being editor of a local newspaper was tricky in a sleepy backwater town. Any small kernels of gossip she embellished, sometimes to a point beyond the truth.

"He deals with things in his own way, does Mike," Dan said, before offering a coffee that Sandra accepted. Rising from his chair, he asked what had brought her to the station.

"Come on, Dan, I think you know. Poor Bill Hicks. What is it that happened?" Sandra said, a flashy recording device appearing in her hand with the suddenness of a magician producing multi-coloured handkerchiefs.

"There's not much we know, right now. It was an animal attack. I've been in touch with the county sheriff and we're taking things from there. As you heard, we'll organise a hunting party. We don't want anything this dangerous roaming near town. We'll be looking to spread the word to exercise caution, of course. But everything points to this being a horribly unfortunate accident and until we have reason to think otherwise, that's how we're treating poor Bill's death."

"And what do you say to the rumours that you were warned about a dangerous animal lurking near town?" said Sandra, barely pausing to take in Dan's first response.

"Bill's death is not linked to any contact we have had recently. I won't say anymore on that," Dan replied. If he'd put Jim Jacobs in a cell for the day like he should have then he'd only have half a headache this morning.

"Do you think your inexperienced police department has dropped the ball here, putting Loomis citizens at risk?"

That was the final straw for Dan.

"Enough. I have work to do. Out, please, now."

Without any complaint, Sandra walked out of the station, a smirk on her face. Several people walking along the street stopped and stared, and a few faces appeared in store windows too.

Dan knelt down by his desk, opened the draw, and pulled the emergency packet of cigarettes sellotaped underneath it out. Stepping outside into a cool breeze, ignoring the eyes fixed upon him, he lit a Marlboro and looked up Main

Street and out towards the heavy forests surrounding Loomis. What the heck was out there?

***

By midday, a small hunting party had gathered in the street outside the police station. Mike was stood next to an older woman, squat, with red hair tied into a ponytail. She wore camo trousers, boots, and a t-shirt emblazoned with her store's name, 'Lee Hunting Supplies'. It was a longstanding family business. Sally was as close to a matriarch figure Loomis had; people were always calling on her for advice. She nodded at Dan and called the group to gather round, then began passing out high visibility jackets to be worn over the clothes. A good way to prevent everyone shooting each other.

"Thanks for coming. I'm sorry we're here, but of course you've all heard about poor Bill Hicks. We believe we're looking at an animal attack. Probably a large animal, a bear maybe. We'll be splitting into two groups, Deputy Bryant will lead one with Sally, and I'll lead the other. Proceed with extreme caution, keep in close contact with each other. We've got a lot of ground to cover. Thank you."

Dan stepped down from the porch steps of the station, just as a red truck pulled up outside. The door opened and slammed shut. A red-faced Jim Jacobs stumbled onto the sidewalk.

"I warned you," he shouted, his words slurred. "And now Bill Hicks is dead. I warned you and you did nothing. You're a disgrace, Daniel Weathers. And you, Mike… whatever your name is."

Before Dan could respond, Mike strode over to Jim, took his arm, and shifted it behind his back. Moments later a handcuffed, struggling Jim Jacobs was coerced into the station and placed into lock-up.

Mike reappeared a few moments later. "He needs to cool off. Drunk as a skunk and driving round. He's going to kill someone one day."

A few murmurs from the gathered hunters, many of whom barely knew Jim, quickly quieted. With that, the group set off for route 7. From there they would enter the forest, heading in opposing directions. They'd scan the perimeter and work their way in deeper.

***

By late afternoon it was beginning to go dark. The hunting party had returned to the police station, shaken hands, been thanked for their efforts, and headed home. Only Sally remained with Dan and Mike.

"It's real strange, is all I'm saying." Sally had been grumbling for most of the afternoon. "Pass me one of those cigarettes, Dan," she demanded. Dan passed her one and said nothing as she lit up inside the station. "Must be the full moon, it does funny things to nature. Unnatural things. Strange day. Not a single sign of anything," Sally continued, shrouded in smoke.

"Can't say I'm too surprised," said Mike, lying back in his chair and placing his size 14s on his desk.

"It don't feel right. A violent animal attacks someone in town, actually comes into town, and we do a big sweep by the afternoon the same day and nothing? I don't get it, that's all."

"I'm not surprised," shouted a voice from the cells. Jim Jacobs was listening to their conversation.

"Get some rest, Jim, you can go home in the morning," Dan shouted back.

"Aye, and by then Bigfoot will have killed again," Jim said, banging his hand against the cell door.

"Bigfoot?" Sally said, looking to Dan with a smirk on her face.

"Now you know why we didn't take Jim's 'warning' seriously. We aren't looking for a man in a monkey suit, we're looking for a bear," Dan said. He lit a cigarette and took a deep drag from it.

Sally rose, grabbed the box of high vis jackets she'd distributed earlier, and said goodnight.

"Get yourself home too, Mike. I'll bunk up here and keep our distinguished prisoner company. I'm too tired to do anything more tonight and, frankly, there's nothing we can do."

Mike nodded and grabbed his bomber jacket. As he opened the station door, the light of the full moon illuminating the street, he turned to say something, then paused. A guttural howl split the silence of the evening. It was a deeper cry than that of a wolf and neither Mike nor Dan recognised it.

"This town, man," Mike said, shaking his head.

***

Flames flickered between the old guide and his enraptured audience. It was slowly getting darker but passing cloud cover blocked any early signs of the moon or stars. The romantic mood the campers were expecting had yet to materialise.

The guide pulled out a stick of beef jerky and gnawed on it like a dog.

"You see," he said, still chewing, spittle forming around his dry lips, "what you don't know about Bigfoot is this…" He paused, swallowing his masticated food. "Bigfoot walks among you. He ain't a shy animal hiding in the wilderness, he's part man, part beast, and he hides in plain sight. You hear?"

The group laughed uneasily, spurring the guide on. Seeing the effect of his words was like taunting a bull. Quiet settled in the clearing where they had set up camp. Rustling and hooting broke the temporary peace.

"But where's Bigfoot?" one of the young women cried, hugging her boyfriend's arm tightly, the silence getting to her.

"Oh, don't you worry, he's coming," the guide said, offering a wide yellow smile.

***

Dan awoke fully dressed, lay on the grey couch in the station, covered by a worn blanket. It took a moment to adjust and realise it was someone banging on the door that had stirred him. Casting aside the blanket, he rushed forwards, strapping his belt and holster in place, and turned the key. Sally Lee damn near knocked Dan over as she pushed her way in.

"Happened again," she said, breathless. "Goddammit, it happened again. You got a real problem on your hands here, Chief Weathers."

Dan, startled by one of the townsfolk referring to him by his title, looked at Sally in bemusement, his tired brain unable to process what was happening.

"Hector is sat inside my store, shaking like a dog shitting pinecones. Round back of his bar, the scene he described... You got another animal attack, Dan. A real bad one. And it don't make no sense to me. We covered a lot of ground yesterday and saw no signs of anything, so how did a bear sneak back into town unseen? This ain't no bear. Ain't no bear," Sally mumbled, grabbing the cigarette packet from Dan's desk, passing him one, then lighting them both up.

Dan thought back to the footprint at the scene yesterday. Was that only yesterday? Dan shook his head and rubbed his eyes with his spare hand, then took a deep drag of his cigarette.

"I'll call Mike en route," he said, "please, Sally, show me the way."

***

Mike was inside the bar with Sally and questioning Hector. Or maybe just comforting him.

Dan had called the county sheriff again and requested the medical examiner be sent back up this way. They had no place to store a body, let alone assess wounds like the ones he was looking at. Head caved in. Entrails spilled forth and, seemingly, eaten. Bite marks littered the body. The lower left leg had been twisted nearly back-to-front.

It was a small parking lot that served Hector's bar. By the bar's backdoor were a row of large waste disposal bins, stacked full almost to overflow.

"Could the smell have attracted an animal? It's pretty out of the way," Dan muttered to himself, walking the perimeter he'd taped off. At least this scene was hidden from Main Street.

Sunrise offered better light as Dan stood and stared at every aspect of the car park, every piece of trash, every mark on the concrete ground, every nicked fencepost. He'd placed a sheet over the body, not wanting to look at it any longer.

Just when he felt like giving up, something caught his eye. A clump of black stuck around the wire fencing that marked out the parking lot. Dan approached like it was a bomb that could blow with the slightest vibration of movement. Slowly, he plucked the clump of black material from the fence. It was animal fur.

Mike came out through the backdoor and shouted over to Dan, who pocketed the fur, and wandered over, dipping beneath the police tape demarcating the scene.

"Hector is real messed up. Says it's Manny Rojas. He'd been in the bar last night, left at closing, and that's it. Didn't hear nothing, didn't see nothing. This is getting weirder, Dan. I can't stop thinking about Jim Jacobs…"

"I'm gonna stop you right there, Mike. We are not giving any thought to Jim Jacobs beyond whether or not we charge him with driving under the influence. I've called county, the ME can be with us later today. Until then, we're gonna need to secure this scene, no one in, no one out. Sorry buddy, but I'm gonna need you on watch duty. I assume Rosita was with Manny last night?"

Mike nodded a yes.

"Those two were inseparable, so where is she? Let's find out if she saw anything. She works at the dental surgery as a receptionist, right? I'll head there. I can look up next of kin later. Hey, Mike, look at me. This was an animal attack, okay? It's bad luck. I gotta go, I'll update you when I have something."

Dan turned, leaving Mike stood by the lot, a white sheet covering the mutilated corpse of Manny Rojas. As Dan walked away, the clump of black fur felt heavy in his pocket.

***

Rosita had failed to show for work that morning, so Dan headed round to the apartment she shared with Manny, her twin brother. The apartment was situated above Loomis Sporting Goods, so Dan walked around back and clambered the rusty staircase. He was about to knock on when he heard a wail from inside. He tried the door, which was unlocked, and stepped in.

"Rosita," he called, "it's Dan… Chief Weathers. Are you alone?" Dan's trembling hand hovered above his gun holster.

The apartment was small but neat and tidy, decked out with family photos and Christian paraphernalia. Another cry startled Dan. He inched forwards. Spots of blood stained the carpet. Dan pulled his gun from its holster and proceeded up the hallway. He pushed open the bathroom door, announcing his intention to enter and who he was once more.

Rosita was stood with her hand in the sink, running it under the tap. Blood swirled around the bowl, but her hand was half-hidden, and Dan couldn't see the injury. He holstered his weapon, seeing no threat. No one else appeared to be in the apartment. Rosita cried out once more, before turning to Dan.

30

"Please leave, you shouldn't be in here," she said, her voice weak and hoarse. "It stings so much."

"Rosita, what happened? I need to speak to you about Manny. Rosita, Manny is dead. I'm so sorry. But please, let me take you to the doctor to help with your hand."

Dan tried to take a closer look at the wound, but she turned away.

"I don't need a doctor. Please leave me alone, please!" Rosita shouted. Her face was streaked with make-up, tears, her own black hair, and blood. She clearly hadn't slept or changed clothes from the previous evening. Dan noticed blood and water splashed about the floor and walls.

"What was it that did this to you?"

"I cut myself on broken glass. It's nothing, it just hurts. I don't know anything about Manny. Just leave me alone," she repeated. With this, she wrapped her hand in a towel and charged at Dan, shoving him back and shepherding him towards the lounge and, gradually, towards the door.

"Okay, Rosita, okay. I'm going. If you need to talk, please call me at the station."

Dan considered one last plea to accept an offer of help but, before he could open his mouth or lift a hand, the door had slammed shut in his face. Stood at the top of the steel staircase out in the cool autumn air, Dan closed his eyes and exhaled.

Before Rosita had covered her wound fully with the towel, he'd caught a glimpse of it.

It was a bite mark.

***

"They were teeth marks, Mike. I asked Doc Mason to call on Rosita, but he tells me she wouldn't let him in," said Dan, slumped in his office chair. He'd just got off the phone with the Rojas's father; the second tough conversation he'd had to have in as many days. This job was meant to be a breeze. You do your rounds, keep the local kids in check, break up the occasional bar fight, and more or less lend a generous ear. You were the man about town, a respected, paternal figure. Quickly, Dan's tenure was slipping into nightmarish territory.

He looked out the window and saw people filing past. They shot glances into the station, caught Dan's eye, and quickly turned away. The sky was overcast – during the rainy autumns Loomis suffered the capricious whims of the weather. One minute bright sun, the next torrential downpours.

"Do we need to start thinking about this big beast that Jim saw?" said Mike, who'd finally been relieved of his watch once the ME had collected the body. Mike saw Dan wince at the mention of Jim Jacobs. "No, hear me out. Look, I'm not saying Jim Jacobs is a reliable witness. I'm not even saying he's describing what he saw accurately. But we've got a weird report of a large unknown creature right by town, and we've got two grisly deaths in the next two days. It has to be connected. And this ain't no Scooby Doo shit, where Jim Jacobs is going round in a monster costume. He's been in lock-up overnight, for a start."

"You should listen to your deputy, Daniel," shouted a voice from the cells.

"Goddammit. Mike, can you caution Jim, give him his last warning, and throw him back in his truck."

While Mike escorted a grumbling Jim Jacobs out of the station, Dan took a moment to look online. Loomis wasn't exactly a modern metropolis, but people used social media. One of the things he'd implemented when he took over was adding a couple of social media accounts, just to bolster the police presence. When he logged in, he saw his notifications were through the roof.

'*The police don't know what they're doing. Who's next?*'

'*You can't expect a kid to run a police department*'

'*They're hiding something from us – CONSPIRACY*'

The messages went on along those lines. Some tagged Dan's account, others he searched for. It felt strange to be referred to as a kid, given both he and Mike were thirty. But the worrying aspect was the idea they were hiding something from the public. He'd set up social media and tried to keep up the rounds his father had done because he wanted to be as transparent as possible.

Dan remembered the clump of hair still stuffed into his trouser pocket. He thought of the footprint, and the teeth markings on Rosita's hand. Dan lay his head on his desk and closed his eyes.

***

It had been over two weeks since Manny's death. Sandra had written a scathing article about the attacks and laid the blame firmly at Dan and Mike's door. It didn't matter that it didn't make sense, it caught on with an audience broader than Loomis Creek and that alone spurred Sandra on to continue writing whatever brought her the most attention. Jim Jacobs hadn't helped matters, bumbling around town spilling his story to anyone who would listen. And Nancy Hicks had arranged Bill's funeral for the following week. She had asked Dan and Mike not to attend.

They sat in the station, staring at the walls. They hadn't made their rounds all week. The atmosphere in town was feverish. Glares slashed at them like knives, each one cutting deeper.

Dan noticed the ME had finally emailed over the autopsy reports and clicked into it disinterestedly. Scanning the words, row after row, Dan tensed up, felt his body shaking. He reached for a cigarette, a habit he was now fully reinvested in, and lit up. Mike noticed the change in demeanour and walked round

34

to take a look at his computer screen. Moments later, he fell backwards, catching himself against the wall.

"How is that possible?" Mike whispered.

"I don't know," Dan replied, "but I think we need to open a murder investigation."

"It's a mistake man, it has to be."

"I don't think so, Mike. No animal DNA was found on the bodies, but the same human DNA was found on both. It's awful, but this can work in our favour. We can become heroes, man."

Mike remained in thought, stood over Dan's shoulder. He folded his arms, still leaning against the wall.

"I think we should…" Mike began, before looking up to see a man he didn't recognise walking up the porch steps.

"Excuse me fellas, I understand you're the law around these parts?" the man said, holding the door open. Parked outside the station was an older black Chevy with tarpaulin covering some bulky equipment in the back.

"Er, yes, I'm Chief Weathers, this is Deputy Bryant. How can we help you?" Dan said, while Mike made his way back round to his desk.

The man shut the door behind him and strode across to the couch and sat down. A young man, maybe mid-twenties, he had long blonde hair tied behind his back, a tan fedora sat on top of his head, and wore hunter's garb, all dark greens and khaki. But his necklace stood out. A simple black band around his neck decorated with teeth. Human teeth.

"I understand you had a couple of attacks at the last full moon?" the man said, in a manner suggesting he was well aware of what had happened.

Dan's eyes narrowed and he glanced at Mike before answering. "There were two tragic deaths, yes. An investigation is ongoing."

The man nodded and smirked. "Interesting. I suppose you don't have any evidence it was an animal attack? I'd suppose you're thinking you've got two grisly murders on your hands? Seems odd to me that a serial killer would do two in two days and then just stop." The man rose from where he was perched on the couch and stood between the two officers. Looking from one man to the other, he smirked again. "Any other strange goings on?" he added.

"Cut the shit, man," said Mike, jumping from his chair. "Who are you and what do you know? I'll arrest you right here for wasting my time if you don't start talking."

"I don't take kindly to threats, Deputy Bryant. I'm here because I know what happened in your little town of Loomis Creek. If you want to know, I suggest you take a seat."

To Dan's amazement, Mike eased back into his seat. The man had a soft, quiet voice, a slow drawl. But despite his relative youth, there was an authority behind his words. Few people put Mike Bryant in his place.

"Well then?" Dan asked.

"You heard of the Lummi? A Native American people of Washington. The Lummi used to speak of Ts'emekwes. Peaceful creatures, shy, reserved. Mostly found in mountainous forest areas, thick bush in which they could hide. There are plenty of different names across the world too, with different lore. Commonly, you'll know them as Bigfoot."

The man let this final word hang in the air. Faces stared into the station from across the street, no doubt their attentions garnered by the battered old truck sat outside. Dan rose and walked to the windows, closing the shutters.

"Sceptics, eh?" said the man. "I understand. It's outside of your experiences or understanding so you find it hard to believe. Ineffable is the word – too great to understand. Well, you better had, because the stories about peaceful creatures are total BS. At the full moon, when they transform, these beasts hunt."

"What do you mean transform?" said Mike, eyes wide, fixed on the stranger.

"These creatures hide in plain sight. For most of the month, they're human. What I'm saying is this: your killer is someone in town."

The Loomis Herald's office was just off Main Street. Small and simple, adorning the walls were framed newspaper clippings and photos of various Loomis luminaries, often seen shaking hands with Sandra, smiling awkwardly. The office faced route 7 and Bill Hick's now desolate autoshop. Sandra stared out of the window at the empty forecourt, so often full of cars, now a haunting reminder of the violent end Bill met just beyond its borders. She startled at a firm knocking on the door.

"Dan, what can I do for you?" she said, her tone over-friendly.

A gust of wind following him through the entranceway, Dan stormed past Sandra without so much as a glance.

"Who the heck have you called in, Sandra? I've got a fella called Jeremiah sat in my station telling me I need to set up a network of sniper nests ready to shoot Bigfoot on sight."

"I've done what you should have done in the first place. I've taken heed of Jim Jacobs's warning and contacted someone experienced in this area. He's a young man but his family have a long and, when I did some digging, storied history with creatures of this kind."

"You're sticking your nose into police business in a desperate attempt to boost your career," Dan yelled, jabbing a finger towards Sandra.

"And you're just plain desperate," she replied, temper flaring in response to Dan's aggression. "You've got a town of people who think you're sat on your ass hoping this whole thing goes away. I spoke with Nancy Hicks yesterday. Speaks very highly of your father. Says he'd be turning in his grave at the thought of the Chief of Police being held in such contempt."

Dan slumped into an oak chair by Sandra's desk, his head in his hands. A clock ticked loudly on the wall behind him.

"Sandra, we got the autopsy reports back. No trace of any animal on them. We're looking for a human."

"From what Jeremiah has told me, they could be one and the same," she replied, grabbing two mugs and starting up the Nespresso machine.

"I can't, Sandra. Can you imagine what people would say if I told them we were hunting for a person who turns into an 8-foot-tall monster every full moon?" Dan replied, accepting a warm mug.

She nodded in response, glancing out the window at Bill's empty forecourt once again. "I understand the position you're in. And I know you think I'm making trouble. But this is my town too, and I think something sinister is going on. When I started looking into this crazy idea of Jim's, and I hit upon Jeremiah and his family history, I started looking at similar cases. There are plenty across the country, but the Pacific North West is a veritable hotbed. And you know the type of towns often hit by these violent, mysterious deaths? Fishing towns, hunting towns. Places where you see lots of transient footfall.

"There's a pattern. It's the full moon, Dan, all of these violent deaths happen in three day spurts at the full moon. Jeremiah insists he's been hunting a particularly violent Bigfoot for some time. Please, just give him the time of day. If nothing comes of it, then so be it. But at least you'll have tried."

Dan looked out the office window at the forests extending beyond view, thinking of the difficult terrain, rocky, dark, treacherous. He blinked and pulled his vision back inward and scanned the various photos on the walls of famous men and women using the town as a photo opportunity, the grinning face of Sandra next to them. Maybe it made sense that the monsters weren't out there. They'd always been among them.

***

The walls of Hector's bar were dark wood panels. Its low ceiling leant it a claustrophobic air. Eyes had followed Dan and Mike from the moment they'd entered, as if waiting for them to transform into wild beasts. A serenade of hushed voices dogged their footsteps. A man they didn't recognise, haggard and grey, was perched on a barstool.

"Let me get those, barkeep," the man said, placing a handful of dollar bills on the counter just as Hector was passing the two police officers their beers.

"That's not necessary…" Mike began, but the stranger held up a filth-encrusted hand.

"I think it is. You boys got a lot of undeserved flak these past weeks. I'm only a wilderness guide passing through, but I can see you're just two locals trying their best. Seen the same types in my hometown, just honest folks. Hope things turn out well for you," the man said, sinking the remainder of his beer. He patted Dan on the shoulder and limped towards the exit. As he did, Jeremiah walked through the door. For a second, both men stood at odds, hesitating, before the stranger bowed his head and walked out.

"You wanted to speak with me," Jeremiah said as he approached, taking no notice of the old man who had just left.

"Let's take the corner booth," Mike said.

Bad Moon Rising by Creedence Clearwater Revival played on the jukebox. Curious eyes continued to follow the officers, especially now they were meeting the 'monster hunter'. Rumours spread fast in a small town and they tend to take on a life of their own. Hence, Jeremiah had quickly become the monster hunter. In turn, the town began to believe there was a monster that needed hunting.

"Look," said Dan, his eyes examining the person sat before him. He still wore a fedora but had shifted to full army combat trousers and a black fleece. His eyes were bright blue and his face youthful, which Dan had trouble reconciling with a supposed reputation as a hunter of mysterious beasts. "I don't know what

41

happened to Bill and Manny. I don't think I believe we're looking for a monster. But the whole town seems fixed on the idea that something is amiss, and they don't think Mike and I can handle it. We've got a murder investigation with nothing to go on but two victims that look to have been killed by animals. We've got an autopsy report telling us that the evidence doesn't support that theory. You see how I've got a big hole of missing information in this story?" Dan asked, a frantic note lacing his words.

Jeremiah nodded, his eyes moving from Dan to Mike and back again.

"Now I have you, Jeremiah. The mystery man who tells me he can fix things and give me the information that plugs the hole in the story. So, as Chief of Police in Loomis Creek, I'm asking for your help."

"We've withheld one piece of information," Mike said, leaning forward as if a conspirator in a treasonous plot. "Where Bill was killed, we found a footprint in the mud. Easily twice the size of a human print. We didn't know what to make of it… so we kept it quiet. Why freak people out?" he added.

"And that's not all," said Dan, shifting uneasily. He pulled something from his pocket, something Mike had yet to see. "I'm sorry Mike, I should have shown you this straight away." Dan placed a clump of black hair onto the table, sliding it over to Jeremiah. "From the second crime scene."

Jeremiah picked it up, thumbed it, sniffed it, then placed it in his chest pocket. "These kills were bold, right on your doorstep, in the middle of town. That tells me this is an experienced Bigfoot. He enjoys killing. And the footprint, the hair, coupled with the location of the kills, tells me he's taunting you. Heck, you could have spoken to them already. These guys will stick their nose into an investigation, for sure," Jeremiah said, placing his hands together before him.

"The hunting party?" said Mike, turning to Dan.

"It's possible," he replied.

"I'd say likely. Now there's only one way to kill a Bigfoot in its transformed state and that's a silver bullet. If you get me a good vantage point, I can take this thing out. I just hope it'll get careless. There's a good chance it knows I'm here now, so I could have spooked the bastard," Jeremiah added solemnly. The necklace of teeth around his neck shone strangely in the dim light of the bar. "We wait until full moon, then we set up cameras. You want evidence of this if you can get it. The film can be grainy, so people dismiss it as fake, but I'm hoping over time to build up a catalogue of evidence that's irrefutable by any authority. Anyway. In the meantime, you fellas get back to normal. Make your rounds, answer questions, tell people the investigation is ongoing. When it's full moon, we're gonna kill this son of a bitch."

***

Evening drew in and darkness fell across Loomis Creek. After an awkward conversation in which Nancy Hicks called him every name under the sun before conceding there was hope for him yet, she had given Dan permission to use Bill's

43

autoshop. Situated at the far end of Main Street, it had the perfect view along the busiest part of town. Perched on top of the office roof, Jeremiah had erected a sniper nest, borrowing grey blankets to cover the frame and blend into the grey stone building.

"And now we wait," Jeremiah muttered.

Time passed and the narrow strip quickly went quiet. Occasionally, someone would step out of Hector's bar. Otherwise the night was quiet. Behind them the noises from the forest kept them company. Rustling, snapping branches, animal cries. In between, silence.

"Do we do this all night?" Mike asked, knowing full well the answer was yes.

"That's the plan, said Dan, night vision scope to his eyes. The one bonus of being a police department amid a broad wilderness was access to equipment useful for tracking in the dark.

There had been no movement down Main Street for upwards of an hour and they were onto their third flask of coffee. Mike's head was bobbing, and Dan too was struggling with tiredness. He shook Mike awake and passed him a drink. Jeremiah was as eagle-eyed as he had been four hours ago, his rifle's scope scanning for its target. Suddenly, the rifle stiffened, and Jeremiah adjusted his position.

"We've got something," he whispered.

"I can see," said Dan.

By the side of Hector's bar, around the corner of which was the car park where they had found Manny's body, a figure stumbled out.

"Drunk?" Mike asked, a note of frustration in his tone.

"No," said Jeremiah, taking in a deep breath.

Through their night vision goggles, cloaked in deep green, Mike and Dan saw the human figure slowly edge into the centre of Main Street. And then the person convulsed as if hit with a jolt of electricity.

"Is that Rosita?" Mike muttered.

"Holy shit, it is," Dan said, thinking of the distressed woman he had left bleeding in her apartment, the woman who had lost her brother, the woman he couldn't help.

The convulsing figure of Rosita bent down, her hands against her head.

And then they heard her scream.

It was an agonised cry, as if she were being tortured. Her outline quivered. She stood upright and gazed upward towards the full moon. And then her body began to grow. Limbs extended and thickened, her torso and legs expanded, and her clothes tore. Finally, her head widened, and her jaw protruded out. For a moment, the figure that had been Rosita fell to its knees as if in prayer. And then it rose to its full enormous height.

Its next cry was not a scream, but a roar that shook windows and rattled doors.

The beast, for there was no other way to describe what Rosita had become, stumbled forwards, still appearing drunk.

And then the rifle exploded.

Dan and Mike clutched their ears to stop their brains leaking out, such was the painful ringing in their heads.

"It doesn't make sense," Jeremiah muttered, though the two police officers were unable to hear him.

Gradually, the pain eased, and the two officers climbed down from their perch along with the monster hunter. He carried his reloaded rifle as a precaution. The body of Rosita lay, in human form, naked in the street.

"I don't understand," said Mike, reaching down to check for a pulse.

"They transform back into human form when they're killed. It's like nature's failsafe, another way to convince you the Bigfoots aren't real. But you know what you saw, and we'll have footage to show people. But it just ain't right…" Jeremiah said, laying his rifle on the ground.

"What do you mean?" asked Dan, watching Jeremiah pull a wrench-like tool from his pocket.

Jeremiah stooped over Rosita's body and looked at her now dead face. Using the tool, he reached into her mouth and yanked out a tooth. He wiped it clean of blood and pocketed it.

"It don't make sense" said Jeremiah, "because she seems green. She was wearing clothes, for a start. You saw them rip off easily when she transformed. It sounded like she was in pain, and her movements, the way she stumbled about, were the movements of a confused animal. But like I told you, we're hunting experienced prey here."

Dan saw the full moon above. He looked about his town – he saw a couple of people emerging from the stores they lived above, the commotion and noise drawing them out – and he made a choice.

"Jeremiah, I want to thank you on behalf of Loomis Creek," Dan began, holding out his hand. Mike and Jeremiah both stared at him, the sudden formality seeming incongruous to the situation. Slowly, Jeremiah took his hand and shook it firmly.

"You've done us a great service. We had two grisly deaths and we have our killer," he said, gesturing towards the body of Rosita lay naked on the ground. He failed to look at her. "I'll be sure Sandra knows what happened and she'll be happy to run this story in full. Your heroics, the beast, the solving of a double murder. I think our work on this case is done, don't you, Deputy Bryant?"

Mike scratched his head and looked at the few townsfolk edging further up the street. Slowly, he nodded. "Yeah, yeah, thanks for all your help," he said, patting Jeremiah on the back.

"I'm telling you, something isn't right here," Jeremiah said, bending down to pick his rifle up.

"You have your tooth, Jeremiah, and you have your footage. There's nothing left but the paperwork and the press. Let us handle it from here," Dan said, cracking a smile and leading Jeremiah in the direction of the police station. Turning his head as he walked, he shouted back to Mike. "Deputy Bryant, could you please secure the scene?"

And under the silver light of the full moon, Mike set about his work. He could only hope they had handled things right and the episode was at an end.

***

The four young campers swapped glances and stared at the old guide. Darkness had now fallen on the camp. Clouds still drifted across the sky.

"I thought this was like the seventies?" said one of the young men, his arm around his girlfriend's shoulders. He looked across at his buddy.

"I did too until they mentioned social media. Lemme Google it," said one of the girls. She pulled her phone out, but quickly pocketed it. "No bars," she muttered.

The guide stood up and ruffled his dirty grey hair. He took his jacket off and placed it where he had been perched. Then he kicked his shoes off. The young campers watched with curiosity at this odd action.

"Jeremiah did indeed think there was another Bigfoot on the loose. No doubt he's still trying to track him. Dan Weathers is still Chief of Police in Loomis. Mike Bryant, well, he resigned just a few weeks after the events I have spoken of. Something just never sat right with him," the guide said, pulling his jumper over his head and tossing it to the ground.

"Hey man, it's cold out here. What are you doing?" said one of the young men, standing up. The others quickly did the same, glancing nervously at each other.

"You see," the guide said, ignoring the question, "the Bigfoot attacks in Loomis Creek happened just a couple of months back."

Unbuckling his belt, the old guide started to laugh. It was a dirty, hideous laugh. As he laughed, the sound deepened. Throwing off his t-shirt, the old man stood naked, and looked up at the sky. The clouds dispersed to reveal the glow of the full moon. Eyes yellowing, the old guide's body exploded before them. Hands and limbs elongated, hair sprouted from pores, his jaw extended, his teeth sharpened. A tremendous guttural roar rocked the trees surrounding the camp, and the Bigfoot attacked.

Widow

"Don't be afraid, miss, I'm not here to cause thee trouble."

A stranger emerged from the knot of trees beside the road, his watery eyes shifting from garden to house to Katherine's sturdy form with the keen gleam of a sparrowhawk.

"You came from the forest?" Katherine asked, eyes passing over its unwelcoming shadow, gnarled trees, shifting shapes.

"No miss, the road. Thought I saw something in there, so wandered in a stretch, but too thick is the bramble. It's not safe in them woods. Anyhow, I come from the town by the bay. Thou know the one," the man said, approaching with caution. Older by a good decade or more, his face wore its years like scars. His doublet and felt hat were ragged too.

"I know it."

"News reached us of poor Martin. We are sorry to hear of his passing, God rest his soul."

"I must be getting on, sir, pray pardon me." Katherine turned her back on the man.

"At the bay it is a small settlement. We have many men and few women," the stranger continued, removing his hat and offering the garden an admiring glance. "Mighty useful you'd be, and I am sure there would be another man with whom to raise a family. And, of course, to protect thee."

Katherine paused to consider that last, ponderous sentence.

"I can smell the rain coming on. Fare thee well." Katherine ducked indoors, bolting the door behind her.

The stranger gazed into the forest, eyes rolling across its trees, then closer, surveying Katherine's garden, sturdy wooden house, storeroom, and cornfield.

"There is something awry in these parts. Pray remember me," he muttered before setting off up the road.

***

Someone passed by the window.

Katherine stared at the shutters. Thin, wiry threads, knit tightly together, glistened in the corner, with a spindly shadow passing across it. Katherine thought it admirable, but let the distraction slip from her mind. Foolish, so it was, to have left the shutters open at night. Thin strips of moonlight tethered her to the bed and orange embers diminished slowly in the hearth. Sweat formed beneath her armpits and her heartbeat surged, ringing like a cow bell.

Katherine held her breath, eyes closed, and tried to focus her senses, but her hand instinctively pawed at the empty space beside her. She smelled the decaying hay of her mattress and noted it needed changing. Nearby crops fluttered in the gentle breeze, and, yes, there it was: the light squelching of footsteps outside her home. Who could possibly be calling on her in the middle of the night?

The footsteps stopped by the bolted door. Katherine desperately wished to grab a knife but dare not make a sound. She slid out from the blankets and crawled underneath the bed. Breath held. Chest tight. Something scuttled over her leg, and she shuddered as it tickled her calf. Katherine bit down on her lip so hard she tasted blood. A spider scurried away.

Katherine lay on the cold stone floor beneath her bed, alive to the chirping of crickets and walls groaning with the agony of compression and decompression. Minutes passed lying in wait, in expectation, of a stranger entering her home.

But they did not.

Katherine heard nothing more that night.

***

Katherine reached out a hand for Martin, but it passed through him as if he were mere vapour hovering in the air before her. She knew then she was dreaming, but the smell of fresh rain on muddy woodland ground gave her a sense of reality, immersed her in the terror of suspension between one place and another.

Martin roamed on ahead of her, his axe resting upon his shoulder. His footsteps gradually became tentative, careful, those of a child lost. Katherine longed to hold him once more, for him to hold her as he did, but the dream would not allow that, would not let her touch him; here, she could only observe.

Martin reached a clearing and in that clearing was a stump upon which he placed the axe. He knelt before it and bowed his head as if in prayer, though it seemed such an unusual place for him to do so given the damp, leafy forest floor. A tall tree at the end of the clearing had within its trunk a chasm, a long slit like a serpent's eye, and as Martin whispered words unintelligible to Katherine, balls of light would appear in the darkness. One, two, three, four, five, six, seven, and, finally, eight. The light was warm and inviting. Katherine moved forwards, drawn to it, but as she did so Martin disturbed as if hearing a noise he could not place, glancing over his shoulder with urgency and grasping his axe close once more. The balls of light faded and, as they did, so too did the scene before Katherine.

***

A crow, settled upon the thatched roof, startled, and flew away as the screaming started.

Dawn filtered through the window and Katherine crawled out from beneath the bed, an unnatural heaviness having woken her. The smell of damp woodland buoyed her briefly, such a delightful and intoxicating aroma, but its charms fell away with an aching she felt in her lower half. She sat up, reaching down to massage her feet, but it was not the touch of human skin her fingers found.

Covering both of Katherine's feet was a hard, crust-like material; translucent, like a frozen lake in winter.

What witchcraft was this? Had some creature stolen in during the night, hidden deep in the forest during daylight, to cast upon her a wicked spell? Katherine's breathing steadied, throat settling after its exertion.

The stranger's words came back to her.

Protection from what?

Surely not? If a member of the settlement possessed such evil abilities, they would soon find themselves dragged before a court or even put to death.

Perhaps this was an ailment, or a test from God himself? No, she was far too humble for such attentions.

Katherine rose, eyes swollen and watery, and dressed, choosing her red waistcoat and matching skirt, with a white coif and shift. She struggled to pull her shoes over her feet, bulbous as they were with their strange encasement.

"Our father, who art in heaven," Katherine scrunched her eyes closed. She paused, feeling the warm and familiar sensation of tears rising. Once again, Martin came to her in the darkness.

Shivering feverishly, Martin's face shone in the candlelight. His hand clasped Katherine's and he leant forwards, struggling to whisper some final words to her. "I will see thee again, Love, when your time to enter the light of our Lord

comes." With this last rasping breath, he fell back onto the pillow and his grip
loosened, hand falling limply aside.

But she could not yet rejoice knowing he was in a better place alongside the
heavenly father. Loneliness weighed heavy as a stone pendant around her neck.
Taking a deep breath, Katherine continued with the Lord's Prayer.

After a small breakfast she tended the garden where parsley and an array of
root vegetables grew. But the stiffness of her feet made movement difficult; she
soon conceded. Katherine regarded everything they had built. The log pile stood
beside the house, hidden from the road. Embedded in the stump, the axe Martin
once used for chopping wood gleamed with threat, but also a strange inertia. Behind
the house lay dense, treacherous woodland filled with animal life—wolves, boar,
and bears roamed free. Deeper within its dark heart hid spirits and entities they did
not wish to disturb, things whose influence they feared may one day extend beyond
that woodland realm. They had prayed for safety every day, which made
Katherine's dream all the more surreal; Martin would never have ventured so far
into the forest alone. Would he? Stories of unsavoury practices in the area were
rumours of a long dead past. So they had thought, anyway.

Martin was an adequate trapper and hunter, and a capable enough farmer too.
Their storehouse, built beside the main abode, was full of barley and oats. The corn
patch was prosperous, too, and they sold well at the nearest town. Martin moved
them to this remote spot, reasoning the land was too hard nearer the coast, but here

it was soft and fertile. He listened to the advice passed on by natives—they called themselves Wampanoag, travellers with feathers in their dark hair; though Katherine was fearful of these dark-skinned strangers, Martin embraced them, conversing through a translator—and planted three different crops. If one failed, the others might not. He had been right. Every step of the way, he had been right.

And now he was gone.

"This here is called daub. Thy hands mix clay, soil, and grass in with water to form a thick paste and you cover the wattle with it. Once set, thee hath sturdy walls." Martin smiled and let Katherine help as he built the home they would share together.

A cool breeze sent ripples through her crops and brushed a wisp of hair across her eyes. As Katherine flicked it away, something in the forest caught her eye. A glint. Something glassy or wet. Or, rather, several glassy wet things. Eight or nine, perhaps. But just as quickly as they appeared, they disappeared.

Three men were walking along the road, still far off but heading in her direction. If the stranger was returning here so soon, their situation must be far more desperate at the settlement than he initially disclosed.

Despite the heaviness of her feet, Katherine shuffled inside and bolted the door behind her. She closed the window shutters, disturbing the intricate webbing, and slid down, back against the wall.

Seconds felt like hours. Tears welled in her eyes. All she wanted was to be left alone.

A trickle of something fell down her face and landed on her shoulder. Glancing down, she recoiled. The spider, its home destroyed, hopped from her person, and scurried across the rough stone floor, slipping between a crack by the wall. Knowing things lived within the walls always discomforted her, and these walls were thick like tree trunks, sturdy like them too. But oddly unnatural, the shape too determined, too deliberate. They would keep out strangers.

"How now, Miss Katherine, I know you're in there."

It was him again, of course. She knew it would be. His eyes betrayed a malevolent persistence she was familiar with, a look that betrayed many a man.

"I am resting after a morning's work and do not currently wish to take visitors," Katherine shouted.

"Miss, our settlement is in great need of women. The population will not survive at the current rate. Please reconsider, why not join us in returning to town? I know a lovely young man with good prospects who is in need of a wife. He will look after thee. Living here alone… these forests, they aren't safe."

Hushed conversation followed this, as if an argument were taking place the other side of the wall through which she listened, the wall that listened with her, held things in its memory. Katherine glanced at the bolted door.

"I just wish to live my life here in our home. Good sirs, leave me in peace."

The door clattered. And again, though the bolts held firm. It would take more than three men to break in without a weapon of some sort.

"Please don't find the axe. Please, please don't find it," Katherine held her breath. She knew it should be stored away, but since Martin passed, she couldn't bring herself to touch it, knowing his rough and calloused hands were the last to grip its handle being some oblique comfort.

"I have asked nicely," the stranger called. "Open up, else I will return with more men, fully prepared to break down this door. I do not wish to make threats, but my hand is forced Do not push us, Miss Katherine."

Katherine's hands traced lines upon the hard casing of her feet while she cried silent tears. The door clattered two more times. Desperate shoulder charges, but unable to break through. Soon, the lingering quiet indicated the men had departed. They would be back.

***

A fire roared for it had been well fed. Katherine checked the door was bolted and the shutters firmly set, then climbed into bed.

The crust-like casing around her feet continued to creep up her legs, hardening as it went, until she could not bend her knees. If she focused, she could see it knitting its way upward, a cold and clammy coat. It reminded her of the daub

Martin used to set the walls of the house, except the casing around her legs was covered in tiny hairs imperceptible to the human eye. Only through stroking the surface of the casing could Katherine determine the ticklish sensation was due to the flicking of fine hairs. They did not comfort her, though she grew enamoured with the feeling.

All afternoon, when not stroking the rapacious growth, she thumbed the crucifix Martin had carved for her, praying she would not lose her legs. How would she tend her garden? How would she harvest the crops if unable to stand?

Rumours of low birth rates were rife in the New England settlements. Women of birthing age were in short supply and some men snatched them where they could, be they settlers or natives. She knew the stranger would have his way eventually. She could not hold out forever, was not master of her domain, merely tangled in the corner of a web, praying to go unnoticed by the malevolent creatures patrolling its threads.

The idea of being with any man but Martin revolted her, brought her out in shivers and goosebumps. The tension gave her a headache, one which only subsided with sleep.

***

Katherine awoke with the first blow. The sound was distinct. A brief whistle, then a short, sharp gadunk. Silence. Whistle. Gadunk. Someone was chopping wood.

She reached for the carving knife on her bedside table.

Pain shot through her legs when she tried to move them, the casing covering up to the stomach. Searching fingers felt the reverberations of the material's creation, felt the quiver of threads rapidly knitting together, growing at an exponential rate.

Soon, Katherine would be entombed.

Whether it be this rapacious sickness or the strange man, some malign fate beyond her control awaited. Katherine bit her lip until it bled again, holding back a scream.

Silence. Whistle. Gadunk. And then nothing. Eight times this unknown person lifted the axe and eight times they brought it down and split its target in two. But was it the watery-eyed stranger from the settlement, or someone else? Some*thing* else?

Katherine concentrated, inhaled deeply, and flung herself off the bed, hitting the floor with a heavy thud. A cry spilled forth, but a morbid resignation soon settled her once more. It suited Katherine better to join Martin in heaven. If the axe were to crash through the door, she would welcome it, and welcome its embrace as her attacker lodged it in her skull.

"Our father, who art in heaven, hallowed be thy name," Katherine whispered, closing her eyes. Over and over, she recited the Lord's Prayer, but no further sounds were heard beyond the chirping of crickets and the creaking of desolate forest.

***

By morning, Katherine's body was fully encased within a glassy white exoskeleton, so tightly enclosed she couldn't help but remember the crossing from England on the Mayflower. Packed in like hay within a mattress, sleep hard to come by, they'd survived it together. Sickness, death, rough seas... And now here she was, unable to move, trapped alone in a coffin of unnatural design, a coffin within which she would no doubt rot alone with nought but memories of warmth to sustain her. Her vision dimmed, only shapes and colours discernible. Little light found its way in, the shutters closed. She felt the cold.

A tremendous crashing noise shook the house. Someone was charging the door and it shuddered with another forceful impact.

No one person could break it down.

Through the milky shell, Katherine could make out shapes, but little else. At the third clatter the door swung inwards, bolts hitting the floor somewhere across the room. A dark figure entered her home. It surveyed its surroundings with hands on hips, then slouched over to where Katherine lay. The figure knelt and placed a hand on Katherine's head, though it could not reach her flesh. Fingertips brushed the casing, then it stood and backed away, quickly departing.

Exhausted, Katherine passed out.

***

A narrow, vertical fissure appeared on Katherine's torso, from stomach up to chest. First, a thin crack, no more than a hair's width. Kicking with all her strength, some deep instinct instructing her, the fissure widened, and she poked black stubs through it. The funnels of her mind had multiplied, controlling more elements than before, but with no additional strain. She felt strong and kept pushing. One, two, three, four, five, then six, and seven, until eight black, hairy legs thrust forth, further widening the fissure until, with a final exertion, they shoved open the hard casing. A wider scope of vision assailed her, threatened to overwhelm, but adjustment came to her swift and certain.

Katherine climbed out of the husk of her former self and saw with different eyes. The milky white shape of her human form was thin and brittle, would erode and fade, dissolve into dust. Her eight limbs stretched and tip-toed across the room and out the broken door. Her many eyes surveyed the dark forest in which she would forge a new home, one spun from deep within herself.

"When you are lost, I will lead the way. When I am lost, I trust thee to lead me to the light. This I promise to thee, Katherine." Martin leant forward and kissed her on the forehead. Standing before their newly built home, Katherine wept with joy.

Perhaps now Martin could rest.

"Oh Miss, I warned you I'd be back… By the devil, what's happened?" a voice cried. The squelching of footsteps preceded a man passing by her garden.

It was the stranger.

He was not alone.

Katherine crept forward, eyes seeing many tinted versions of the man. He fell down and backed against the wall of the house, eyes emitting a fear he'd no doubt seen in Katherine. Her eyes were different now. The man cowered, muttering prayers as she placed her legs about him, planting them against the wall. Screams and cries of witchcraft distracted her a moment. A group of men, the stranger's posse, put together to kidnap an unwilling woman. Such bravery, she thought. The men dropped their pitchforks and hammers and sticks and ran away, flies fleeing from her grasp.

She leant over the stranger, the man who thought it fit to threaten her with his 'protection', and droplets of saliva slid from her fangs, landed on his head. A stench of sweat and urine. Katherine squealed and hissed inches from the stranger's face, then skittered away, leaving the man to stew in his own fear.

The warmth of the sun cossetted her as she surveyed her home and garden, remembered the happy memories of Martin and the safety she'd once known.

All was still. Only the snivelling, anxious inhalations of the stranger could be heard.

Katherine lingered, then set out into the forest.

Pay the Toll

Headlights approached for the first time in… he couldn't remember when. Bright circles like two staring eyes, their yellow irises merging into a single broad beacon. He clambered out from his hiding spot beneath the old stone bridge, stepped into the dirt road. A backward glance at the concrete leviathan, the cause of his solitude.

"What the hell are you doing?" A man jumped out of the car—a flashy BMW—and stormed toward the bridge, a shadow slicing through light.

"Pay the toll," he droned above the yawning of motorway traffic.

"Jesus, you're one ugly son of a gun! You're huge!" said the BMW driver. He adjusted the dinner jacket he wore and squinted at the enormous figure blocking the bridge. "What are you?"

"I troll. This my bridge. To cross, gotta pay toll." The troll brandished a tree trunk as a club and raised it above his head. In truth, he didn't need it to pulp a human, but it looked the part and kept his hands from getting bloody. Once the red stuff seeped into the crevices of his knuckles it was impossible to wash out.

"I don't pay to go anywhere. I'm lost, truth be told, supposed to be looking for Brandywine Cottage to meet a, er, friend. You don't happen to know the way, do you?" A sly smile raised one corner of his mouth.

The troll sighed and dropped the tree trunk with a clatter. "Back past cow field. Turn right. You not afraid me eat you?"

"I'm Tommy Treadwell, son, I don't get scared of nothing. You're a big chap though, what you doing skulking beneath this nowhere bridge?" Tommy pulled a cigar from his jacket pocket, lit it with a silver zippo lighter, and took a puff. "Stinks of exhausts and shit."

Tommy Treadwell was the first visitor to the troll's bridge since the motorway flyover had been completed. The troll sighed a sound akin to stones clattering down a mountainside.

"Me troll, Mr Treadwell. Too big for world."

"In my world, big is useful." Tommy flashed a pearly grin, a shark smile. "You need to do yourself a favour and drag yourself out from this bridge, get yourself a proper job."

The troll sighed again and ogled his own feet. What was he doing here? Upholding some promise to his father. Scaring travellers into paying the toll. Threatening to eat them alive.

Humans weren't really on the menu, though.

Not that many passed by anymore.

"I got a job."

"Hell, this ain't the kind of job that'll get you ahead in life. This is just a Sisyphean nightmare you're living out."

"This all I know. You got job?"

"Well, that's not quite what I meant. What experience have you got other than sitting under a bridge and threatening people with that tree trunk?" Tommy puffed on his cigar and blew smoke rings, little grey circles that gradually dissipated like childhood dreams.

"Never done other job," the troll said. Rocky joints crunched against each other as he bent over and plonked himself down on the ground, eye to piercing grey eye with Tommy Treadwell.

"Then you've got to work harder. Graft will get you everywhere, you can take that from me. I'm a self-made man, you know? Never took nothing from no one, just scrapped my way to the top. There's nothing more satisfying than knowing you did it on your own."

"Where to start, Mr Treadwell?"

Tommy stepped toward the troll and looked him up and down, grabbed his moss-covered chin and assessed the monstrous specimen the way a farmer might a prize-winning pig.

"I'm going out on a limb here; I want you to know that. Okay, okay, come work for me. I've got an opening for a doorman at one of my clubs and if there's one thing you can do, it's look big and intimidating. Listen, I'll have one of the boys come down with a van in the morning, pick you up, bring you to a safehouse." Tommy Treadwell dropped the cigar and stubbed it out with Italian leather.

The troll watched the cigar's light die. A tempting offer, a real job. Long ago, he'd enjoyed the smell of the fields and the stream and the trees, but they'd been replaced by exhaust fumes and burning rubber. He nodded and took Tommy Treadwell's manicured hand in his stony, moss-covered fist.

***

The black coat and black woolly hat were specially made to fit the troll's enormous bulk. Stood beside a brightly lit door, the troll presided over a small queue of men, old and young, stood in the Manchester drizzle.

"Jesus you're big, ain't ya?" said one man as he stumbled out of the gentleman's club.

"They dig you up from somewhere?" said another, stubbing out a cigarette then sauntering past.

Another man, too drunk to enter, proceeded to throw a punch at the troll. One broken hand later, he found himself flying fifteen feet along the alley and clattering into a pile of black bin bags. Rats scattered from the wreckage.

Car horns bibbed from the street and revellers' voices rose and fell like the screams of the drowning. Fear faded fast for humans once they didn't sense threat.

The troll spent his nights watching the humans carefully, almost all eyeing him first with suspicion, then derision, then ownership. Almost always they grabbed his arms or patted his back, all the while swearing or calling him names that seemed not pleasant.

This was exactly as Mr Treadwell warned. Drunks and freaks, a circus from which there was no escape. But it was a steady job and Mr Treadwell had given him a room in an old warehouse of his because it was the only place he could fit in. And that right there was the thing he struggled with: fitting in. Despite standing several feet taller than any patrons of Mr Treadwell's club, somehow *they* looked down on *him*.

Loud beeping from the street caught the troll's attention, and two yellow circles moved toward the entrance.

He stepped forward and raised a thick arm. "No cars down here, mate."

Tommy Treadwell emerged from the brightly lit doorway wearing a pinstripe suit over which was draped a vast sheepskin coat. An unlit cigar hung from a hand bedecked with gold rings. "It's okay, troll, he's here to see me. But I need your assistance for this little meeting, so come stand behind me."

"Yes sir, Mr Treadwell," he said, sidling behind the boss as the car slowed to a stop.

The driver stepped out and opened the back left passenger door.

"Tommy," a jovial voice called. Out from the car came a man dressed in similar fashion, but the tailored suit failed to hide the frail body beneath it. A diamond-topped walking stick propelled the moustachioed man along until he stood before Tommy and the troll. "Jesus, Tommy, are you picking up staff from the quarry?" The man chuckled at his own joke and shook his head. "What's it come to that we can't even meet in the civility of your club? Stuck out here like hoodlums, rats. It's unbecoming."

"Don't make me laugh, Sylvester. All sense of decorum went out the window when your boys decided to shake down two of my laundrettes."

"It is… regrettable. A little over-exuberance on the part of a few young idiots trying to make a name for themselves. How is Mavis? I'm sorry the boys scared her," Sylvester said, bowing his head, genuine remorse further creasing his pale face.

The troll tried to follow the conversation. Tommy complained about disrespect often, and he'd ranted and raved about a theft just a couple of weeks past. A full brandy glass had shattered against a wall, the victim of his rage.

"I don't care how Mavis is doing, I want to know how you plan to repair the damage to my reputation, Sylvester. Am I the kind of man to let something like this slide? I haven't been in the past." Tommy stepped toward Sylvester, turned his head, and spat into a puddle.

"Now, now, Tommy. I understand you are upset, but we have always got along just fine in the city and I do not see this should affect our relationship. I have transferred the monies owed to the account as you instructed. Now I would prefer to bury the hatchet." Sylvester leant forward and held out his hand, which trembled with the fragility of old age.

"Was it your grandson who robbed me?" Tommy asked, eyes dropping to the hand hovering between them.

Sylvester exhaled deeply. "It was."

Tommy nodded, his mouth a thin strip, jaw terse. He reached out and accepted Sylvester's hand.

***

"I showed a lot of faith in you, wouldn't you say, troll?" Tommy crunched on an apple and raised his eyebrows. Sat across the table in his dimly lit warehouse, the troll perched on the breezeblock sofa he'd built himself. By the window, a bed of flowers grew toward the light. The smell reminded him of home.

"Sure, Mr Treadwell, I appreciate everything you've given me. I'm working hard to do what you ask and honour that debt."

"Debt is an interesting word to use, troll. Interesting. I'm glad you see it that way. I scratch your back, you scratch mine. You remember Sylvester, yeah? Old fella, wispy moustache, looks like a Poundland Hugh Hefner?"

72

The troll nodded and glanced about at the books and magazines he poured over in his spare time, appreciated what he'd built here.

"Well, on the subject of debts, Sylvester considers a debt he owes me to be repaid. But I don't see it that way because I've taken a hit to the intangibles, if you catch my drift? Reputations are hard earned and easily shattered. You like living here, right? We're friends, aren't we troll?"

A tightness settled in the back of the troll's neck, an awkward crick.

The troll nodded a yes.

"One of the boys will pick you up tonight in the van and you're going to sort something out for me. Sylvester's grandson, Mario, is a greasy good-for-nothing who needs teaching a lesson. I think you're the guy to do it. I want his legs broken off and I want you to eat them in front of him. Do you hear me?"

"Mr Treadwell, I don't know if—"

"It sure is a nice little home you're building here, troll. You're enjoying life, helping yourself out from the gutter. Learning to read, well, you surprised even me. Look at you, doing so great. Sure would be a shame to curtail that, er, upward trajectory." Tommy let this statement hang in the air, his straight mouth a flat line saying nothing more because nothing more was needed.

The troll glanced at his books and plants once again, then nodded agreement.

***

From the darkness of the van, voices could be heard. One was laughing and joking, youthful. The other serious, gloomy. One of the voices knew what was coming as moonlight slipped in through the opening van doors.

The troll unfolded like Optimus Prime and grasped the shirt of the young man, yanked him up to eye level. The two bright orbs widened, drinking the troll in.

Around them a sombre graveyard of abandoned, broken down trains and strips of overgrown rail tracks silently watched on. Nothing stirred among the hollow metal corpses. But the screams of the young man, all signs of youth eviscerated, replaced by a grotesque mask of fear, pierced the night.

"I'll pay you anything, please, just let me go! It was an honest mistake, that's all!" Mario cried, wriggling like a worm on a hook.

The troll swapped a look with Tommy's other guy, who slipped round the side of the van and climbed back in. He didn't want to see the show.

"Mr Treadwell doesn't like people taking his things. He's a man of reputation and reputation means everything." The troll parroted the phrases and words of his boss, sharp angular things cutting his tongue as they rolled off it. What does a man think of himself? What does a troll believe? A moss-covered, stony hand wrapped itself around Mario's soft leg and tightened its grip.

"Please, oh God, please, no!"

It didn't matter what he believed, the troll thought, all that mattered was survival.

His eyes met Mario's again and, in that split second, they reached a gruesome understanding.

***

The troll scrubbed and scrubbed with a scourer and bleach, rinsing it off at intervals, but the redness shined between the hills of his knuckles. Sighing, he dried them with a ragged towel and loped over to his living area. The tap on the sink whistled from the corner, shrill and tired.

The troll glanced at his bookshelf, at his flowers, then to the high ceilings of the warehouse he'd made his home. A mobile phone rested on the table, a gift from Tommy. It started to ring, Tommy's name and number showing on the illuminated screen. No doubt he'd been informed of the successful little operation they'd pulled tonight. On the drive home, the troll's colleague expected hostilities to escalate between Tommy and Sylvester, a genuine turf war the likely next step. The troll had nodded along, only half understanding why a war was necessary.

The phone continued to ring. The troll reached for it, red lines glistening between his knuckles, and hesitated. He could leave. He could go back to his bridge, or find another job, or do anything else.

Except he couldn't.

He owed Tommy Treadwell.

He answered the phone.

In at the Deep End

"It's so lovely to finally meet you, Shaun. Carrie has been hiding you away for too long! But nothing *untoward* has happened, right? This one seems… *strong*."

Carrie's mother smiled with more teeth than the human mouth should, by rights, contain. An effusive smile, but not warm. By contrast, her father sat at the head of the table with a stony stillness not seen since Rodin hung up his chisel. Shaun noticed his shoulders shake and wondered if he was ill or simply holding in hatred for his daughter's new boyfriend. Carrie routinely threw Shaun apologetic glances.

"Mother, please…"

"What, dear? Good food, good company. A perfect Sunday, I'd say." Her voice was girlish, over-sweet. Given Carrie's description of her parents, Shaun had expected to be eaten alive, so the awkward yet polite dinner they'd enjoyed so far was perfectly acceptable. Though it didn't stop him glancing at his watch.

"Could I please excuse myself to use the bathroom?" Shaun asked, placing a napkin beside his empty plate. A sense of being in the way of the conversation – some shadow lurking in the depths – told him to take evasive action.

Carrie's mother lifted a long pale hand to point upstairs. "Second door on the left, my dear."

Lamb and gravy scented the air, competing with an enormous John Lewis candle he'd been informed upon arrival was a Sunny Daydream. Holding his breath as he left the dining room, Shaun trudged up the steep, narrow steps. A series of awkwardly staged family photoshoots adorned the walls. As Carrie grew older in each photo, her parents stayed the same. They hadn't aged in… twenty-eight years?

The bathroom smelled strongly of disinfectant, and the odour spilled down his throat. Shaun hurried up, desperate to leave the cloying space. A shaggy blue rug lay in the middle of the floor. Shaun's foot skidded forward on it, flipping him backwards. He landed in a heap with his arm jammed beneath him.

"Are you okay, Shaun?" Carrie shouted in response to the *thud*.

Through gritted teeth, Shaun replied he was okay, and hauled himself upright with his good arm. The right hand dangled like live bait, an earthworm on a hook – a broken wrist, for sure. His watch still worked, but he didn't dare attempt to remove it. Nausea fell in waves and sickly warmth shot through his veins. Of all the times for something like this to happen, why the first time meeting Carrie's parents? She'd delayed and delayed this meeting until, finally, Shaun pushed for it. He figured something in her past triggered her reluctance. An abusive ex, perhaps? Carrie refused to talk about exes at all.

He groaned, swallowed down the shock and pain and embarrassment, knowing he only had to survive dessert, and descended the stairs.

Fresh spoons and bowls decorated the table. Shaun sat down and lay his broken wrist upon his leg, wincing as he found a comfortable spot. Across from him, Carrie raised her eyebrows and mouthed: 'are you okay?'

"What time is it, Shaun?" Carrie's mother interrupted, nodding at his wristwatch.

"It's… Oh gosh, let's see." Shaun delicately placed his good hand beneath his wristwatch and lifted it toward his face, pain rising with it. "Quarter past five," he spluttered.

"Erm, thank you, Shaun. It wasn't too trying a question, I hope."

Shaun blushed and stared into the depths of his apple pie. Just keep going, ignore the pain, he thought, and you'll get away with this.

"Could you pass the cream, dear?" Carrie's mother asked, smiling at Shaun.

"Sorry?" Shaun asked. Paranoia pushed a strange thought into his head: Carrie's mother was deliberately targeting his injured hand.

"The cream, dear, it's just on your right."

"Right. The cream. To my right." Shaun rose a little from his chair, squatting like a toddler over a potty, and reached across himself with his left hand to pick up the cream and deposit it awkwardly in front of Carrie's mother. Even her father's eyes followed each jaunty movement with morbid fascination.

"Um, thank you, Shaun. Anyway, Trevor, you were talking about work?"

Spoons clattered with dishes and cream and apple pie slurped down gullets. Shaun struggled, but ploughed on, focusing on not dropping anything. Each tiny sound felt heightened, as if he were having an out of body experience. He tried to tune back into the conversation. Had Carrie's father not heard his wife?

"It's the same every year," Carrie's father declared suddenly, "the weak and the meek are identified and politely asked to leave. A business cannot function to its optimum capacity while carrying dead weight."

"Human beings," Shaun said without thinking. He couldn't believe he'd spoken out of turn and whipped a hand up to cover his mouth.

The right hand.

"Aaaaargh!" Shaun screamed and jumped up, bashing the table with his knee and the bowl with his good hand. Apple pie and cream hurtled through the air and sploshed all over Carrie's father. The statue remained unmoved. Apart from the eyes, two bullets aimed at Shaun's chest.

"Oh Trevor!"

"Oh my god, Shaun!"

Carrie leapt up and tried to coerce Shaun from the dining room. She instinctively reached for his right hand.

"No!" he cried, flinging his wobbly haddock of a hand aside. "Aaargh!" Pain pulsed from the broken bone and ran up his arm. Finally succumbing, Shaun held his limp right wrist, cradling it like a new-born.

"Oh no," whispered Carrie, standing back. "Not again."

"Not again? Caz, what are you talking about?" Shaun said, voice wavering with pain. Sunny Daydream enveloped him, producing whole new levels of sickness. Carrie was staring with muted horror, but not at Shaun. Following Carrie's gaze, Shaun caught sight of her stricken parents. Had he given her father a heart attack?

"In the wild, the weak and the injured are picked off," growled Carrie's father, rising from his chair. Cream dripped from his nose. A long, searching tongue wiped it clear.

"You've hurt yourself, dear. Such a shame. Things were going so well," Carrie's mother said in that saccharine tone of hers. But the eyes were jet black, unblinking, fixed on Shaun's wrist. All those teeth stretched beyond the confines of her mouth. She placed a hand on the back of her chair and turned to Carrie. "Darling daughter, could you fetch the bucket, mop, and disinfectant. We'll be needing it."

Carrie turned to leave.

"Carrie, what's going on?" Shaun cried. Both parents transformed before him, jaws widening into razor sharp smiles, skin morphing to scales. He cradled his arm and backed toward the wall.

Carrie paused in the doorway but said nothing, then disappeared upstairs.

"The weak cannot survive in the wild." Trevor and his wife rounded the table to descend upon dessert.

Invasive Species

It was the green glow creeping in through the curtains that had Cassie restless. Something the size of a dog scuttled around their pond. Bright green and frog-like, but a giant frog, a frog you could put on a lead and take for a walk. It shone like a nightlight.

Cassie crept out of bed and pulled on her dressing gown. Slipping downstairs, she walked through to the kitchen and faced the patio doors. All glass, the entire garden visible in daytime. But at night, a suffocating wall of black.

The bright green outline waddled in a circle. Cassie hunted for the key that would allow her to slide open the wide glass door.

"There you are," she said, grabbing the key from beside the fruit bowl. Turning back to face the garden, the luminous creature was gone, swallowed up by the jaws of night. Cassie's nose and breath smudged the glass, eagle eyes searching for its re-emergence.

Nothing came.

***

"Can you water those geraniums, love?" Cassie's mother, blonde hair tied into a ponytail, was on her hands and knees, big yellow gardening gloves on, sharp shears in hand, attacking a rosebush she'd wanted to dig out for months. She wore denim overalls, Cassie a comfy yellow sundress. Her mother wiped sweat from her

83

forehead using her wrist. Summer was peaking, but the heatwave spelled disaster for the garden. Or so Cassie kept hearing.

"There was something in the garden last night," Cassie said while pouring water over the plants. Ever since dad left, her mother had become strangely fixated on the garden. Cassie didn't really understand why, but she liked to help, if only to keep on her mother's good side. Days like today were the best. A strong scent of flowers on the air, a gentle hum from the pond. A cooling breeze.

"Probably an owl." Her mother strained, yanked at bulbous roots. An earthworm poked its head up through the sea of dirt and debris.

"I think it was an alien. Or a mutant frog. Like the ninja turtles, but from space." Cassie continued pouring water until the flow slowed and stopped.

"Maybe you were dreaming, hun. You'll need to refill the watering can. In this sun, we can't risk the plants drying out and dying."

"I wasn't dreaming, I really saw it. I got out of bed and came downstairs and saw it." Cassie stood still, glaring at her mother.

"Can you just fill the can up, please Cassie, the flowers need more water. Eurgh, another worm." Cassie's mother tossed the stray worm aside, thankful she'd worn her thick gloves.

"Daddy would have believed me," Cassie said, stomping off toward the outdoor tap.

She knelt down on the patio and turned the tap on, blasting it so she couldn't hear what her mother was saying. She looked upset, though Cassie wasn't sure why. Maybe she knew daddy would have believed in the mutant frog and now mother was ashamed. Daddy used to read Cassie stories and fairy tales before bed, so she knew he believed in magic and strange things. That was before he left.

Cassie struggled back holding the can in two hands.

"You've overfilled it," her mother said. With a sharp yank, a thick root came flying out like a cork from a champagne bottle.

Cassie's mother screamed.

Cascading upwards was a geyser of earthworms, a wriggling shower of dirty flailing limbs. They writhed as if scared. As if escaping some sickness in the soil.

"Get them off me!" Cassie's mother flapped her arms, brushing worms onto the turf, while Cassie did the same around her legs.

"The worms are running away from you," Cassie said. Worms spiralled off across the grass like the panicked folk of Pompeii as Vesuvius exploded.

"I need to shower. I feel like they're on me. Can you finish watering those geraniums, please hun?"

The backdoor slid shut, announcing her mother's escape. Always running away. Never toward. Cassie hovered over the pond. The fish scooted about, pulling together, nudging into one another. Algae made Cassie scrunch her nose up. She

85

bent down and traced a finger along the plastic netting. Of course, she was old enough now to be trusted not to fall in the pond, but the netting remained.

As Cassie circled the murky waters, she came upon something that caught her breath.

A large, fresh hole in the netting.

***

The night was less cloudy, a thin film of light caressing the garden. Cassie's nose pressed against her bedroom window, breath heating patches of steam she'd instantly wipe away.

Cassie blinked tiredness away, squinted at the void. Beside her sat her phone, camera open and ready to snap snap snap. But the garden was still, no unnatural bright lights, no frog-like creature.

Cassie sighed, yawned, plugged her phone in to charge. Lay facing the ceiling, she thought about the times she'd gone frogging with her father. Their neighbour had a pond too, so frogs were always hopping around. Daddy was a tall man, sandy haired. He held a big green bucket and used the tap to add a dash of water for the frogs to lounge in. Cassie always called the frogs they caught Bob. Some were lively, some tense, each had its own little personality. She liked the slimy feeling and the rough skin. Her father would laugh as they picked them out of the bucket and placed them round their pond. He was always laughing.

Cassie wondered, before sleep took her, whether the luminous creature had been a dream after all.

***

One of the koi carp floated on its side; an unblinking eye stared at the sun. It was unsettling, like there'd never been any life in it.

"I'll need to treat the pond… Oh my, the grass…" Dropping the net and running around the pond, Cassie's mother skidded to a halt and threw her hands to her head. The grass around the edge of the garden had turned yellow and dry, resembled straw. A yellow path carved round the edge of the garden like the yellow brick road leading to Oz. But this path led from the bushes and flowers at the bottom of the garden all the way to the pond. As if someone had sprayed the grass with a strong pesticide and killed it.

"I think they're footprints," Cassie said, running her hand along the dead grass. Bone dry.

"It was just the heat, Cassie, don't be silly."

"But you can see the patches where it's not a straight line. Look!" Cassie slammed her sandal down onto the tiny, disparate patches. Each fit the small, slender shape of her foot perfectly.

"I need to treat the pond, Cassie. Why don't you go inside and watch TV?" Cassie's mother began to busy herself with the pond, removing the netting. She paused to stare at the hole, shrugged, continued dislodging netting from the pond's rocky boundary. Cassie, with a forceful harrumph, stomped indoors.

***

Luminous green emerged as if pulling apart the air itself, climbing into this dimension from another. Cassie grabbed her torch and shot downstairs, eked open the backdoor, slipped out into the night.

"I know you're here, Mr Alien," she giggled, padding toward the pond. "So where did you get to? I bet you're really nice and want to be friends. I'll call you Bob, I think."

The bright circle from the flashlight scrolled across the grass, the slim blades of green yellowing in patches Cassie knew to be footprints, no matter what her mother said. Daddy wouldn't just have believed her; he'd be searching for Bob with her.

On the light circle moved, skating along the fences, toward the bushes, round to the pond, a searchlight hunting an escaped convict. Finally, it settled on the water.

Ghastly glassy eyes watched the stars. Scales glimmered like oily water. So many eyes. Cassie counted the dead carp under her breath. Netting lay scattered about, shredded.

Luminous green leapt from the water, pulled Cassie into the pool. Slimy spindly fingers clung tightly to her. She spat out mouthfuls of grimy water, algae and a chemical flavour burned her throat. And there, before her, was Bob. Froglike was about right; scaly skin, eyes dark and bulbous, a reedy antenna flopping from his spherical head. Dead carp bumped into Cassie's hips. Those spindly fingers set her straight, kept her steady. She smiled at the creature and was sure he smiled back at her, offered no threat or malice. The quick padding of quick footsteps on grass, a dread gasp, then a scream. Something clashed with the water's surface, Bob's grip loosened, disappeared. Spray burst around them like the foot of a waterfall. Cassie rubbed dry her eyes, saw her mother swinging something down onto the luminous green form. Bob writhed and wriggled until the blows rained down caught him wrong, caught him on the skull once too often, triggered a few spasms, then a stillness.

Bob floated among the carp, eyes closed, leaking from the head.

Cassie's mother tossed aside the bloody shears, flung herself at her daughter, gathered her up, kissed her all over, told her everything was okay.

Cassie spat out the remains of pond water, coughed until her throat hurt less. "You didn't have to kill Bob, mum, you didn't have to kill him."

Out of the Darkness

It wasn't like Scrunchy to disappear like that, but it wasn't like any of the other dogs either. Maura watched out the rain-speckled window and clung to her stuffed elephant, Flopsy, while scrutinising every set of headlights, every tree branch shaking in the wind, and every sporadic whistle and grunt from along the quiet street.

"Bedtime soon, Maura," her father said, placing the newspaper down on the coffee table.

"But Scrunchy is out there, and it'll be dark soon." Maura glanced out at the grim sky. Further along, the road narrowed into a lane that descended through a stable and onto the meadows where anything could lurk. At least, that's how it seemed to Maura.

"Not this again… dogs aren't afraid of the dark, only little girls. We'll go out looking again tomorrow, okay?" Her father used his firm, 'this is final', tone. Maura nodded quietly.

"Do you think Scrunchy is with mummy?" she asked.

Her father hesitated before rising from his armchair and sighing. Outside, the wind howled like the call of the wolf. "Time for bed, Maura."

***

Maura rolled back and forth before finally kicking the duvet off. She was fully bathed in yellowish light, having insisted her curtains remain open. Outside her window, a streetlight glowed like a beacon. Between that and the pearlescent full moon, Maura's room hid no secrets.

She flung her legs over the side of the bed and rose. On her tiptoes, she leant against the window and pressed her face to the glass.

She gasped and fell back onto the bed.

"Scrunchy," she whispered.

Maura jumped back up against the window and stared down into the street. By the foot of the streetlight, a ruffled Labrador had its leg cocked, and steam billowed around it. Maura giggled, but she stopped as Scrunchy finished his wee and trotted off up the road.

"Come back, boy," Maura said, still quiet, unwilling to wake her father.

She grabbed her dressing gown and tiptoed down the stairs. If she could bring Scrunchy home, it would be a lovely surprise for her daddy and maybe he'd be happy again.

Slipping her Wellingtons on, she eased the front door open and gently shut it behind her. The front garden was dishevelled and the rose bush out of hand. Mummy used to prune the bush and tend the flowers. They'd been left alone for months.

The rain had subsided, but Maura pulled her dressing gown tight around her and suppressed a shiver. Puddles splashed beneath her feet as she hurried out of the garden. A Missing Dog flyer blew into the gutter. Up ahead, she saw a golden tail disappear down the hill.

Scrunchy was headed for the meadows.

Maura scurried after him. Bushes and branches hung over fences flanking the lane. The houses ended and, in their place, an open yard expanded, with stables surrounding it. A horse neighed and whinnied as if sensing Maura's presence. She loved the horses, but they'd have to wait; she couldn't say hello now she was on Scrunchy's trail.

Up ahead was an old gate. Through that gate the path narrowed beneath a canopy of trees that blocked out all light.

That golden tail was swallowed by the darkness.

Maura reached the gate and stared into the abyss.

She took a step backwards and glanced over her shoulder. Daddy wouldn't come out at this time, and he'd tell her off for leaving the house. Maura pulled the dressing gown tight around her again. She wished she'd brought Flopsy along to protect her.

Maura gritted her teeth and strode through the gate.

***

Water splashed with her every step, but Maura persisted onwards. Scrunchy was nowhere to be seen. Shapes formed in the darkness. The outline of crippled hands stretching across the path. Smiling mouths of jagged teeth. The darkness whispered to her. But still, onwards she marched.

The canopy broke up ahead and a flash of gold dashed out of sight. Maura ran, escaping the darkness as quickly as she could. Tears filled her eyes, but she held them back.

She rounded the corner.

Sat in the centre of a small grassy clearing was her Labrador, Scrunchy. A thick clutch of trees and robust undergrowth behind him.

Among those trees, pairs of yellow eyes beamed like headlights.

Maura hesitated. Scrunchy whimpered and barked at her. From the trees emerged another dog, an enormous dog. A German Shepherd. She recognised her; it was Tilly, who belonged to their neighbour. She'd gone missing a few weeks ago. Tilly barked a warning and glared at Maura, daring her forward. Another dog, a little spaniel, stepped out into the clearing, followed by another dog, and another one, until the clearing was alive with gentle yapping and deep guttural breathing. An army of dogs. Familiar dogs.

"Is this… where you're meant to be?" Maura whispered.

The German Shepherd howled, and silence fell. The leader turned and faced the other dogs, her pack, and nodded at them. As one, they turned and slipped back into the undergrowth, fading from sight like shadows under a dying sun.

The German Shepherd waited by the edge of their realm, for this was their domain, their territory.

Scrunchy bounded up to Maura, who dropped to one knee and stroked and nuzzled her faithful pet, recognising this for what it was: goodbye.

A low growl disturbed them and Scrunchy stepped away, yelping one last time at Maura, before racing off into the undergrowth. The German Shepherd retreated last and disappeared like a mirage might disperse into fragments of imagination.

Maura let the tears fall. She'd been holding them back for too long.

***

Walking along the path, the darkness didn't seem so scary, and her eyes adjusted to see those crippled hands were slender tree branches and those wicked smiles were the curvature of thorn bushes. Soon, she reached the end of the path, and passed back out through the gate and into the safety of the light.

Gifted

Vernon Garner wanted to impress his son on their first holiday, but he knew nothing of four-year-olds, let alone his own kid. Ice cream cones and ferris wheels and paddling in pools would suffice, but Vernon didn't want sufficient: he wanted a lifelong memory.

He'd always wanted to go to Thailand.

Chase arrived on Vernon's doorstep six months prior accompanied by a support worker and a police officer. Sat around the oak coffee table in his living room, the police officer and support worker told Vernon his son was coming to live with him. Phrases such as 'next of kin' and 'mysterious circumstances' found their way through growling thunder and the caustic smell of coffee. Vernon's jaw slackened by degree until two rows of stark teeth showed.

No longer was he a *biological father*. He was a *dad*.

Vernon smiled quietly to himself. His thoughts turned to jagged skirting boards and filthy windows and the black mould behind the spare bed; the steep stone steps down the garden patio toward the too long grass within which, twice, he'd spaded an adder to death. Vernon thought about his job. His 'weekend girlfriend'. Karaoke nights at Jimbo's.

Vernon asked about Janae because he figured it was expected of him. She hadn't wanted him in Chase's life, dismissed him as an unfortunate fling with one redeeming feature: Chase. And now the boy his mother had taken pains to keep from him was dropping from the sky into his life. Under the dim living room light, the police officer and support worker exchanged a look, one thick with meaning. The officer removed his helmet and thumbed it awkwardly.

"Janae Griffin is listed as a missing person. We assumed the grandparents would want custody of the boy, but they were pretty reluctant. Janae seems to have just… disappeared. Or, more likely, run off. The door to her flat was unlocked and a neighbour discovered little Chase here sitting on his own playing with his building blocks."

"The poor lad must have been so distressed." Vernon nodded his head sagely, as if this was a given.

"He's not cried a drop, surprisingly," the support worker replied, waving at the motionless Chase, trying to evince a giggle or acknowledgement. The boy glanced lazily at the woman as if to say, why are you speaking to me like a child. Vernon recognised that glance as one his brother used to give him, long ago. He gulped down a glob of saliva and, with it, a rush of nausea, and focused on the boy. *His* boy.

Vernon would think of that night often. Parenthood seemed some tremulous vortex he'd been tossed into. He had no idea.

***

The tuk-tuk wove through gaps in the Phuket centre traffic that Vernon couldn't see and he embraced the breeze as a form of panic control. Chase surveyed his surroundings, brow furrowed in concentration. Car horns blared around them and music shoved out from bars: Thailand's welcoming arms. Vernon clung to Chase, pulled him in tight for fear he'd fall out the side and into oncoming traffic, nestled his face in the boy's thick fuzzy hair. Ever since Chase had moved in, visions of his son's death plagued Vernon. Each new slaughter—always some mistake or error of Vernon's the cause—a graphic, gruesome end. The visions came to him as nightmares, as daydreams, always vivid, always unshakeable in their imagery, as if his eyelids were pinned open and head fixed in place, the old Ludovico treatment. Frequently, water was involved, but Vernon knew exactly why that would be.

Often, he'd find Chase staring at him, grey eyes fixed on him, Medusa ready to turn him to stone.

Vernon shrugged this off. Chase was a small child adjusting to a new home with his father, just as Vernon was a new father adjusting to sharing his home with a small child. Teething problems, he called it. Anyway, Chase's arrival was a gift. He would make it work.

Precisely why a beach holiday would bring a little well-needed happiness to their arrangement. A symbiosis of opportunities meant it was possible. His uncle recently passed and left him a little money, more than enough to cover flights to some distant exotica. And a friend of Vernon's owned a small beach hut on a pretty secluded stretch that he rented out as an Airbnb. He owed Vernon a favour so, after a couple of drinks and some nurdling, he'd agreed to give it him free for a week.

They could hear the ocean as the tuk-tuk turned into a long row of beach houses. Palm trees stood behind the square wooden huts, huts painted light blues and pale pinks and complemented by full gardens. The ocean noises made Vernon feel sick.

They drove a long way down the row—the houses spacing further and further apart—before pulling up at the very end, a dead end. Vernon passed the driver enough baht to cover the journey, pulled their cases into the garden, held Chase by the hand. Standing in the street, they faced their sandy-coloured beach hut. Night encroached, giving it a disused, cold look. A smell of flowers and grass smothered them as they walked up the garden path.

***

Foam-splattered rocks rose to their right and jutted out into the ocean. A heavy sun glared as Vernon caked Chase in sun cream, white streaks smeared across the brown skin of his nose and cheeks. Their arms and legs glittered with bug spray. Vernon swatted at flies; they didn't seem to bother Chase.

The view was spectacular, Vernon conceded, though the mysteries and dangers of the ocean froze his heart. The azure glimmered, thick golden sand separating the beach house from the water. A light breeze tickled them, trailing a briny odour.

They sat in the shade of their house's veranda, Vernon in a hammock with his nose in a book and Chase on the floor playing with a generic action figure they'd bought at the airport. Vernon was operating a 'whatever Chase wants' policy for this one week.

"Play in sand?" Chase mumbled, the first words he'd said since they'd arrived. The bucket and spade were already in his hands.

"Okay, but not for too long. It's too hot to be out in the sun. You don't want to burn." Vernon felt like this was the appropriate answer as he reclined in the hammock and closed his eyes.

Their first six months were difficult. Chase was a quiet, awkward child. They'd tried all sorts, but little inspired a reaction, although Chase seemed to enjoy those films about that young wizard learning to control his powers. A flash of normality, sadly. Not a lot bothered the boy, but it didn't excite or interest him either. This frustrated Vernon because he could never work out whether his son was happy or sad or needed something. Janae had already made it clear how unsuitable a father he was, and his inability to get a good read on Chase only made her words echo on and on in his brain.

He was glad she was gone.

But still, Chase's behaviour concerned him. It came to a head a month or so ago. Vernon noticed his son was sitting facing away from him, in the corner of the living room, focused on something small. In the interests of ensuring Chase wasn't doing anything dangerous, Vernon had hopped up from his springy armchair and shuffled across the room.

Chase was holding a sizeable spider in his left hand between his thumb and index finger, a firm but delicate grip. Its remaining legs wriggled like loose vines in the wind. Chase used his right hand to pluck away another leg from the spider's body, depositing it onto a careful pile on his bare knee.

Vernon had asked what he was up to. Chase looked up at him and laughed.

Incredulous and frazzled, Vernon insisted they flush the spider down the toilet and put Chase to bed early. There was no complaint, no tears or tantrums, only quiet compliance. Vernon crossed his fingers and hoped his son wasn't a budding serial killer. He'd heard what serial killers do to disappointing parents.

***

Vernon awoke with a snort and instinctively slapped away several mosquitoes buzzing around him, squinted away the bright glare. He used his hand as a shield and looked out from the decking, remembered he was on a quiet little corner of a tropical paradise, felt the desire for cocktails and the company of women.

He sat up and gasped. "Chase!"

Vernon leapt from the hammock, stumbling as he righted himself, and sprinted down the paint-chipped steps.

Sand burned his bare feet. He hopped and skipped as if crossing hot coals for a secret initiation. How did Chase even walk out onto this stuff?

And where was he?

The uneven rise and fall of golden sand stretched down the beachfront, waves lapping over it and leaving a flattened, dark indent. A few luxury yachts sailed across the horizon. There was a sandcastle built in the middle of the beach. It had towers and ramparts and turrets, even a courtyard and drawbridge. A moat encircled it. All the parts of a castle were present, almost in a paint-by-numbers fashion.

Chase's bucket and spade sat beside it.

How could he have fallen asleep? Vernon dropped to his knees.

And then it was like the world stopped. Vernon couldn't move, the vicious whirls of a sandstorm drawing him into its grey eye. A wave of nausea flowed over him. Then, pitch black. Then, a thump.

Something coarse and hard against his face. Unnaturally warm, too. He daren't open his eyes. What if something had taken Chase—for he couldn't think of any other reason for his disappearance—and had now moved onto him?

Vernon bit the bullet, opened his eyes. Yellow walls watched him—perhaps this was the beach house? But no, it wasn't. The yellow was dark, gritty, dotted with black and clear bits, like the eyes of a million insects. Vernon ran his hand across it, thought of rough skin and jagged rock.

It was everywhere, too. Lining the walls were outlines of picture frames containing the daubed images of a child's finger painting. The corridor led to a staircase and banister, all doused in the same gritty yellow and an overwhelming odour of ocean and dirt.

Vernon remembered trips to castle ruins as a child, his parents walking he and his brother up and down giant rolling hills—that's how they felt to his little legs—and among clumps of darkened stone and steps through which wildflowers grew. Only here all was this strange monochrome.

This strange prison was built from... sand.

He descended the stairs, began yelling Chase's name. Nothing. A vast foyer spilled out before him, complete with a sand chandelier. A Sandelier, Vernon thought, trying to retain his sense of humour and calm himself.

"Son, where are you?" he cried, spinning on the spot, his vision blurring.

His feet felt thick, sank a little. The ground wasn't hardened like the walls and furniture, it was golden beach. The shade of the structure cooled the sand.

Sunlight spilled in through the open arched doorway and Vernon sprinted outside, feet dipping with each step. Walls like tidal waves surrounded the sandy courtyard. Two towers in the corners had turrets projecting skyward, linked by battlements with crenelated tops. A portcullis clamped down within the barbican. This was a medieval castle, the type that housed lords and ladies and kings and queens, the sight of sieges in times of war.

Or the type from kids' films about wizards.

The sound of ocean waves rumbled like thunder, closer, closer, further away again.

Vernon threw his hands to his mouth to cover the scream rising in his throat. The sunlight died in an instant and bathed the courtyard in shadow. Something gargantuan blocked the sun.

He escaped into the main building and skidded to a halt inside a great hall with impossibly hanging sand banners, decked out with long dining tables dressed with plates and cutlery and candlesticks. Sand gets everywhere, Vernon thought.

"Chase?" he cried before collapsing onto a bench. He lay back onto the table, eyes closed.

The sounds of ocean waves rolling upon a beach could still be heard. Vernon always thought of his brother, Sidney, alongside anything associated with the open seas. This holiday had been a bad idea from the start.

Vernon felt the hairs on his forearms stand to attention and opened his eyes.

Eight glassy orbs were set into the ceiling. The space around them shifted, twisted calmly. The orbs were fixed upon his reclining form. Vernon leapt aside as eight massive furry legs landed on the tabletop with a thud.

Something from *Clash of the Titans* towered over him. Except Vernon wasn't an epic hero decked out in sword and sandals, he was a car salesman in shorts and t-shirt with grit stuck between his bare toes.

Spittle flew from the spider's gaping, desolate maw; it dripped from hungry fangs.

Vernon stumbled, kicked on, ran from the hall, ran from the sound of too many legs scuttling along like fingernails rat-a-tat-tatting on glass. He turned to the stairs, found himself in the corridors in which he'd awoken, kept running without looking back, wondering whether the giant spider still chased him, clicking its way along the grit-laden walls.

He kept taking corners, losing himself in the maze of the castle. He pushed through a door and found himself outside, fresh sun and cool breeze bumping into him as unwelcome strangers. The door clicked shut, its mechanisms identical to an ordinary door despite its sandy make-up.

And there it was, the beach house. *Their* beach house. Palm trees beside the familiar veranda and yellow-painted walls. Vernon turned to face out to sea, heard the cawing of sea birds like the voices of crying children. And then a sickness gripped him, tightened his chest, kicked acid up from his stomach. All the unpleasant bodily responses.

The waves were close. Too close.

Vernon looked out into the burning white glow of the water's surface. Something bobbed atop the waves.

"Sidney? Is that you, Sidney? Come back, little brother, the water is dangerous."

Whatever it was dipped beneath and out of sight. He vomited over the side of the battlements, the projectile landing in a puff of dust down in the empty moat.

He wiped his mouth dry, fell to his knees.

Vernon knew this place. He recognised it. Chase had watched the films rapt, in his quiet and severe way. Vernon had hoped it would help them bond, could be their comfort watch.

And now he'd lost him.

Just like he'd lost his little brother. Those ocean waves were the cries of a drowning child. Vernon took his eye off his brother for five minutes at most. Long enough for his little dinghy to float into deeper water. Long enough for Sidney to topple out of it.

Vernon cried for his loss, knowing he'd failed again. He was being punished by his own son. And he deserved it.

The tide crawled up the beach. Elongated foam fingers groping for his throat.

And then that great shadow coated the castle in darkness once again. A colossal being, human-shaped, blocked out the sun.

Vernon turned to run but froze. Legs coated in hair grasped the edge of the battlements, pulled up the thick grotesque body of the spider. Its many eyes drank Vernon in, contained a malevolence and a… familiarity?

"Janae?" he whispered.

Vernon fell backwards, shuffled along the grainy, coarse ground.

The great spider edged toward him, then stopped. It looked up just in time to see a tremendous dark hand pluck it from the battlements with casual ease. Vernon covered his ears to block out the unearthly screech the creature emitted, like a whistle designed only to drive him crazy.

A bloody leg clattered onto the battlement, splattered Vernon. A grim smell of iron and vinegar, almost. Something sickly coated him.

Dismembered legs rained down amid a sea of hideous squeals that lost their power with each falling limb.

And then the waves hit like a tsunami. Water rushed over the tops of the battlements. Then, a thump. Then, pitch black.

***

Vernon shivered.

He felt the grime of water-soaked clumps of sand on his legs. Salt water lapped over him, slipped into his mouth, caused him to gag and cough. He rolled over and felt the immediate warmth of the sun, then scrambled from the encroaching waves.

"Chase! Chase, where are you?" he cried once again, remembering his situation, regaining his voice.

"I'm here, Dada," came the reply.

Vernon span around, almost splitting the skin of his knees on the sand. And there, holding a bucket and spade, was Chase.

Vernon picked Chase up, hugged him tight. Finally, slowly, Chase hugged back.

Waves tickled Vernon's feet, cool but not altogether unpleasant. Memories of his brother slid away. And then Chase leant away, held out his hand. On his bare palm, a dark form materialised, pushing up through the skin. It sprouted legs.

107

Chase heaved a whimsical sigh. "We need to build a new sandcastle for mummy," he said.

The Potential of Strangers

The following items were recovered from the accused's computer and mobile phone following their arrest. The accused claimed to have no knowledge of the victims or the local legend most often referred to as 'The Strangers'. These items confirm the accused is being untruthful in these assertions.

No physical evidence as to the existence of third-party involvement in the deaths listed in the case file has been found.

These items are presented as such to outline the malign actions of the accused and to establish a clear design.

***

Exhibit A

MSN Messenger Transcript, 17th December 2006

Carly says:

Hey, thx for the add. U okay?

Vlad says:

Fancy seeing you here.

Carly says:

Well, u did add me…

Vlad says:

I thought you might appreciate it more, but I'm willing to overlook that.

Carly says:

Okay, this is weird…

Vlad says:

I'm sorry, I'm sorry! Just trying to be funny and make friends, not alienate people.
Bad joke. I'm good thank you, how are you? You like The Smiths?

Carly says:

Lmao okay. Gd thx, and I LOVE The Smiths, there like my fave band!

Vlad says:

*they're

Carly says:

Huh?

Vlad says:

You used the wrong form, but it's okay. You're pretty enough to let it slide. So, The
Smiths! Did you know Jonny Marr and Morrissey used to write the lyrics and music
separately, so none of their songs comes out sounding too similar? So cool.

Carly says:

That's so kl! My dad was at school with Morrissey. Every1 near me has a Morrissey story rofl!

Vlad says:

You really are very pretty. What do you want to be if you grow up?

Carly says:

Oh thnx bbe! Ur very sweet! I want 2 be a horse vet when I'm older.

Vlad says:

What, like, putting animals down?

Carly says:

That's not my fav part obvs! I luv animals :) but sum need to be put down if they arent rite.

Vlad says:

Fair enough.

Carly says:

Do u go to St Paul's in Altrincham? Maybe I'd recognise u? Y don't u have a profile pic?

Vlad says:

I like to maintain a cloud of mystery mwuhahaha! And I don't go to school locally... I'm actually at college.

Carly says:

An older guy, yh? That's kl. Which college?

Vlad says:

It's kind of exclusive, you probably wouldn't know it. But tell me more about you. Do you have a boyfriend? I'm in the market for a girlfriend!

Carly says:

Lmao, ur a bit wierd, right? But... yes, I'm single lol. It sux, but it is what it is.

Vlad says:

Misspelling 'weird' has got to be the most common mistake in the English language, don't you agree? But like I say, you can get away with anything, I think. In fact, I bet you do get away with everything!

Carly says:

Lol u got me. U got a WEIRD thing with spelling, right? But ur quite funny 2.

Vlad says:

What's your favourite Smiths song? Mine is There Is A Light That Never Goes Out. Something about the tragic romanticism of dying together with the one you love. Do you know what I mean?

Carly says:

That 1 is really catchy! I luv This Charming Man the most, I thnk. Morrissey is such a kl guy, even tho he's a WEIRDO like you.

Vlad says:

You know, some people would find it weird to see someone deliberately misspell half the words they type. If anything, out of the two of us, I could be the normal one. And plastering my bedroom walls with posters of Morrissey could also be considered weird, now we're on the subject…

Carly says:

How did u kno about my posters?

Vlad says:

Was that guess right?! I thought so. I just took a running jump at it. But my point was only to say one person's weird is another person's normal, if you see what I mean?

Carly says:

Oh right lol, yh, I get it. I still thnk ur weird… But I guess gd weird. I really wanna c what u look like!

Vlad says:

Okay, I'll concede. It is somewhat unchivalrous of me. One minute.

Vlad updated their profile picture

Carly says:

Oh! Ur actually SO cute! U got that hot hair thing going, 4 sure.

Vlad says:

Haha I don't know how to take compliments.

Carly says:

Lmao well get used to it! So wuup2?

Vlad says:

I'm actually reading about this bridge. It's… I don't know if I should say. It has a… bad history.

Carly says:

Oh u CANNOT say that n not explain!

Vlad says:

Sorry! I have to go. I'll talk to you later. Maybe then I'll tell you about this little mystery…

Carly says:

U TEASE! Ok, l8rs bbe xx

Vlad is offline.

***

Exhibit B

Copy of message shared – 'copy & pasted' – on MySpace news boards, plus comments. First appeared 12th October 2006. Shared by Carly Richardson 15th November 2006.

DON'T LOOK AWAY!!

That's when they get you, it's when they got Trevor McKaid, why he was never seen again. Manchester-born Trevor was projected all A*s in his GCSEs, had his heart set on sixth form and university. His parents have been searching in vain for him since late summer, but renowned psychic medium Marguerite Spencer has already spoken with Trevor's spirit on the other side. Now, he belongs to The Strangers.

You won't know The Strangers are following you until it's too late. Because they don't follow you in the traditional sense, creeping round corners, ducking behind cars. They follow you *online*. Tracking your Yahoo and Ask Jeeves searches, sneaking into your messenger friend lists. If you aren't careful, The Strangers work their way into your computer and into your life, then they take that life away. Don't believe it? Ask poor Trevor McKaid's parents.

If you don't want The Strangers to get you, copy and paste this message into a new post within 24 hours.

Comments:

Why do u repost shit like this? It's stupid. Kid probably doesn't even exist!

Patrick Hennessey, 16th November 2006

Omg gotta do this too! And Marguerite is legit, she helped my nan speak to my granddad n she said things she couldn't kno!

Samina Siddiqui, 16th November 2006

You're a very pretty girl. We should chat, if this kind of thing interests you.

Vladimir Semenov, 17th November 2006

Delete. This is how they find you.

L3g3nd5 Fan Page, 21st November 2006

***

Exhibit C

MSN Messenger Transcript, 19ᵗʰ December 2006

Vlad says:

Would you like to know about the bridge I mentioned…?

Carly says:

How Soon Is Now?

Vlad says:

Witty. I like it, Morrissey, I like it a lot. What do you know about the supernatural?

Carly says:

Oh, u mean ghosts and stuf? I guess same as every1, u walk thru 1 and u go cold, some are friendly, some aren't. Bump in the night, like old houses. Y?

Vlad says:

Well, those are the basics of ghosts, yes. But I'm talking about demons. Or maybe worse. It's actually still to be determined what exactly we're dealing with here.

Carly says:

I kno the feeling lmao :)

Vlad says:

Am I a mystery to you?

Carly says:

U want to be, don't u?

Vlad says:

Every man wants to be an international man of mystery, I guess. But we're getting distracted. Do you want to know about this bridge or not?

Carly says:

Ok ok ok, go 4 it!

Vlad says:

There's a bridge over the River Mersey, down the meadows near you, and it's—

Carly says:

Oh! I kno it.

Vlad says:

—a flashpoint for supernatural activity linked to these mysterious beings called... Don't interrupt, Carly, this is important.

Carly says:

Well soz Mr Wired!

Vlad says:

WEIRD. It is spelled WEIRD.

Carly says:

Sorry, sorry, I'm dyslexic. It's 1 of those words 4 me, that's all.

Vlad says:

You should have said. I didn't know. Anyway, do you want to hear about the bridge or not?

Carly says:

Yes :)

Vlad says:

Okay. Now, as I was saying, this bridge is a flashpoint for supernatural activity. The beings in question are known as The Strangers. Little is known about them, but from what I can find they travel along water networks and drag people into the abyss. And there's speculation they're evolving, finding new pathways to take more victims than ever before.

Carly says:

W8, I'm sure I've seen that name somewhere… Summat on Myspace, yeah, that was it. 1 of those chain mail things. I copy n pasted it cos, u never kno…

Vlad says:

Yes, I saw that, actually. Do you not remember? No matter. They've found their way online, it seems. I wonder how these entities will develop and reinvent themselves in the age of computers… But I wouldn't place much store in chain mail. They can, on rare occasions, have something to them. Most are a crock of shit, though.

Carly says:

Lmao, ur so funny! U spk in such a posh and interesting way.

Vlad says:

Haha, you remember what I said about compliments? Anyway, I think we should investigate this bridge. Try to work out why it's a hot spot and maybe what The Strangers are after or look like. This is proper investigation, Carly. I had a good feeling from you when we first spoke, I think we can make a great team. Do you want to meet me at the bridge?

Carly says:

Well, I've got Bloc Party tix 4 the weekend…

Vlad says:

You have great taste in music, you know?

Carly says:

Oh ur so sweet, thx! I luv music tbh. I'm always at a gig. U should come 2 something soon.

Vlad says:

I like that idea a lot. Yes, let me know. Anyway, the bridge. How is tomorrow night for you then?

Carly says:

Well… ok, but not 2 l8, yh?

Vlad says:

6pm at the bridge?

Carly says:

Okay, I'll c u then :) xx

Carly is offline.

***

Exhibit D

Extract from Blogger.com blogpost by account: L3g3nd5, titled: Legends and Folklore of the Northwest: The Strangers, bookmarked by the accused 23rd July 2006

As with any demonic entity, there is the possibility of shapeshifting: assuming the face or form of a loved one, a pet, or an authority figure. Speculation remains rife among the burgeoning world of message boards and online chatrooms that such entities will adapt and evolve. Just as a username could be any*one*, perhaps it too could be any*thing*.

But what influence could a demon expound in the small, insular world of computer geekery? First, we must expand our understanding of the internet and the breadth of possibilities it offers. Andy Warhol said one day everyone would have their fifteen minutes of fame. Well, one day, everyone will have the internet in their home and a device to access it. As its expansion continues, it will become affordable, fast, reliable, and, eventually, ubiquitous. This is happening already. The question then becomes one of access. For a moment, let us postulate the existence of a bodyless, non-corporeal being capable of travelling through certain conductors or through waves. We then create an enormous web connecting almost every home in the world. Are we not building an illicit network for a sinister and malevolent being to exploit?

You may believe this theory takes too many liberties, makes too many leaps. However, it is this author's firm belief that the rise of the internet will present problems of the paranormal well beyond the scope we have previously witnessed.

This brings me to The Strangers. The Strangers are known to navigate only by waterways, often dragging their victims from bridges or from the banks or shore of rivers, a kind of supernatural hippopotamus or crocodile. In an animal attack, you will find the bloody remains of the victim, whether they be inside the belly of the animal or floating fragments washing away. The Strangers leave no such trace. They drag their victims into the water and absorb them, as if swallowing them whole. Naturally, the covert nature of their approach, the suddenness of their attack, makes them difficult to predict and defend against. Launching their forays from beneath murky waters, The Strangers are symbolic of a fear of the unknown. Venture too near the water's edge and you leave yourself open to potential attack.

It is only through first-hand witness accounts that any workable theories can be formulated, or even offer confirmation of their existence. One man living outside Chester, a Mr K. Warburton, watched in terror as his wife was dragged along a stone bridge by an invisible force, only to disappear over the side and never be seen again. Another, Miss L. Smythe, swears her dog was taken by The Strangers. This attack took place along the banks of the River Mersey, on the meadows straddling Urmston and Sale, two south Manchester towns. Walking along and holding Jonesey by the lead, a sudden violence flung Miss Smythe to the ground and yanked her down the muddy bank. One distressed yelp later, the lead went limp, and her dog was gone. Many more witnesses attest to victims displaying a strange fixation with the water, as if entranced by their own reflection like Narcissus, but these are less frequent in occurrence.

Reports range from across Liverpool, Manchester, Preston, Chester, as far south as Stoke-on-Trent, to Fleetwood and Lancaster in the north. This makes The Strangers a uniquely north-western phenomenon. This is, of course, where I believe these two seemingly separate things, the internet and The Strangers, intersect. If these creatures were to evolve, to find a more potent method of killing, a less easily traceable method of travel, they would become an unstoppable force. They may, of course, open themselves up to modern methods of tracking online activity, leaving their true nature ripe for exposure.

Comments:

Interesting stuff. There are so many entities, demonic in nature or otherwise, that can exploit this burgeoning Age of Connectivity. Feels very much like the end of Planet of the Apes, we finally did it, you maniacs… maybe we didn't blow it up, but we're engineering the downfall of humanity. More and more we're capable of, and will be, hoodwinked online, and the consequences will get worse and worse.

V. Semenov, 7th August 2006

***

Exhibit E

SMS sent from the phone of Carly Richardson to Samina Siddiqui, 6:12pm, 21st December 2006

Hey. Met that older guy I woz talkin about… sorry, u wer right, no more guys from msn! he seems ok but a bit full on. he was stood by the river jus starin in b4. like a statue. i thought he was TALKIN 2 the water at first. might hav 2 ditch soon. i don't get any luck with guys, right?! last few have been such… drips. anyway. can knock on in 20 mins?

xoxo

***

Exhibit F

Transcript of Petra Semenov's televised appeal for witnesses in relation to the disappearance of her son, recorded 2nd January 2007, and saved in Notepad form to the accused's computer the same day

My boy loves ghosts. He would read all those books and watch those silly shows, and we, we thought it was harmless. Sometimes he would sneak out alone at night and we would have to ground him. He would visit places where a ghost was seen or some other silly legend. But he loves that kind of thing, and when your child loves something and it makes them happy you, well, you indulge them.

The night he went missing, he said he was meeting his girlfriend to go ghost-hunting. We didn't, Viktor and I, we didn't know he had a girlfriend. He'd never mentioned anyone before. I thought maybe it was a good thing, for him to get out of the house, to meet a girl, even for silly ghost-hunting. He is stuck on that computer of his a lot, you see. He is a quiet boy. Trusting. Smart and silly at the same time. He is a good boy, please, someone find him. If you know anything, please call the police. Please.

**

Exhibit G

SMS sent from the phone of Carly Richardson to Samina Siddiqui, 2:34am, 5th January 2007

I think I did summat bad, Sammi. Was I wit u 2nyt? I can't remember anythin l8ly

SMS response from Samina Siddiqui, 7:12am, 5th January 2007

U okay bbe? No, u wernt wit me last nyt

xoxo

**

Exhibit H

Notepad note, last saved 27th January 2007

~~Michael Simpson~~

~~Carl Williamson~~

~~Trevor McKaid~~

~~Vladimir Semenov~~

Patrick Hennessey

Perfect Face, Hollow Shell

The small and nondescript advert in the local newspaper, reminiscent of an old lonely-hearts ad from the days before dating apps, caught Bentley's eye.

Artist seeking models, aged 35-50, in the Urmston/Flixton area. Do you want to see the perfect version of yourself? Call the number below.

Bentley set the newspaper aside and struggled up from the sofa. Above the dusty mantelpiece was a wide mirror with a carved gold frame of confused limbs, the fingers of which grasped for something beyond the glass. His ex-wife hated it, so Bentley loved it.

But he didn't love the face staring out from the mirror.

Rough stubble, bags under his watery eyes, a pouch beneath his chin, cheeks sloping south: a face in need of a lift. Ex-wives and divorce lawyers wear you down like a pack of starving wolves on the hunt, desperate to strip your carcass bare.

He'd needed a good deal of alcohol to keep himself sane, something he wasn't convinced he'd achieved. Now, surrounded by unpacked bags, bare floor, and plain walls, in a rented apartment he could ill afford, an overwhelming sense of emptiness lingered. The few friends who hadn't abandoned him told him to look upon this time as an opportunity to do things he wanted to do, be the person he wanted to be, but the haggard fish in the mirror only felt like flopping about helplessly until it died.

The perfect version of yourself.

Bentley picked up his phone and dialled the number from the ad.

***

Bentley placed a pint of Estrella down on the sticky table. Seated up on the mezzanine floor, the lounge and bar area below and to his right, he scanned the crowd, half expecting his wife—shit, ex-wife, *ex*-wife—to be among a gaggle of friends laughing like hyenas or making googly eyes with her young lover. But this was the brunch crowd, only families or the elderly relaxing with coffee and sandwiches.

Bentley glugged mouthfuls of lager.

Saxophone-led jazz ballads played in the background, at a volume level beneath the buzz of chatter. A hint of flowers wafted from full vases dotted about on half-cabinets and low tables. The high wall was stacked with portraits in a classical style, a collage of flawed faces—warts and all—casting an imperious glare over the entire lounge. Bentley wondered why some of these flawed faces were so ugly.

Someone walked into the bar and caught Bentley's eye, someone younger—mid-twenties perhaps, that perfect, halcyon age—with voluminous brunette hair falling down her back, a gorgeous face, stunning figure, all the elements required to give every husband in the place a neck strain. She wore skinny jeans and a navy-blue knitted jumper and knee-high brown leather boots.

Bentley missed his mouth, had to use his sleeve to wipe beer from his chin.

The woman looked up at him and narrowed her eyes, nodded, ordered something at the bar, and made her way up the stairs until she stood before him. Up close? Breath-taking.

"Bentley?" she asked, holding out her hand. "I'm Miranda, we spoke on the phone."

Bentley grabbed her hand and shook, surprised by the firmness, and watched as she dropped the handbag from her shoulder and sat down. How odd someone so young and attractive placed a tiny ad in the local newspaper, as opposed to using social media to find clients.

"Can I get you something to drink?" The words came out breathy and nervous, as if addressing a large audience.

"Thank you, I've ordered a coffee they'll bring up, but feel free to pay for it," she replied, followed by a quaint smile, as if accustomed to such offers. Bentley figured as much. When you looked as good as her, you didn't pay for anything.

"So, you'd like me to paint your portrait? You have a face I can see behind. You'll be easy to bring out from the canvas, for sure. I knew you sounded like a good subject on the phone." Miranda's dimpled cheeks swelled.

"You got all that from me already? Artists see into your soul, I guess." Vivid azure eyes bored into Bentley, unblinking, widening to see him all the better.

A barmaid arrived with the coffee and Bentley dutifully paid for it. Miranda's eyes never left his face; his cheeks flushed with the attention. The barmaid collected empty glasses on her way back downstairs, snaking through tables and whisking them away.

"Tell me about yourself," Miranda said, snapping Bentley back to attention.

"Not much to tell, really. I'm thirty-nine, a business development manager, two kids, got the joints and back of a man twice my age."

Miranda cocked her head as he spoke.

"Married?" she said. Just a single word, but the one word in the English language capable of burrowing into his brain and setting a fire.

"Erm, no. Divorced. Recently," he said, leaning back in his chair, arm resting on top of it, presenting as casual an image as he could manage. The gold band on his ring finger tightened.

"What happened?" Miranda leant forward, her brow forming focus lines, as if the answer to her question could make or break some significant decision.

Bentley paused, threatened by an overwhelming urge to word vomit every last bit of spite held within him. Fingers drummed a beat on the table. He expected to hear his ex-wife laughing it up, joking about him. Instead, a few of the husbands cast envious eyes his way. Bentley held back a grin.

"She left me for a younger model, took the kids with her. Took everything, actually." And Bentley continued talking, revealing the ins and outs of the breakdown of his marriage, the arguments, divorce battles, and so forth. Miranda inhaled it as if gaining vitality from the misery, just as Bentley felt the misery fade with this vital exhalation. After his tale was done, Miranda sized him up, cocked her head.

"I can paint you," she said.

***

A clean-shaven Bentley arrived at the studio apartment above the old Victoria pub on time and Miranda greeted him with a hug, asked him to make himself comfortable, and flicked the kettle on.

Small windows let some natural light into the lounge and kitchen area. There was a stool near the far wall, a full-length mirror to the right, and an easel in the centre of the floor. Paint fumes assailed Bentley. The place was modern with plain magnolia walls and grey carpets, though these were largely covered in paint-splattered drip cloths. Splattered with a lot of one colour in particular.

"You use a lot of red, eh?"

"Just call me the Titian of Urmston," Miranda said, stirring the coffee and adding milk.

"Do you live here or just work here?" he asked, accepting a steaming cup between trembling fingers. He held the mug with both hands, embarrassed; this was like a first date, and he was twenty-one again.

"My life is my work, so both," came the beguiling response, a wicked smile close behind. Miranda looked the quintessential painter in denim overalls and a white t-shirt.

"I didn't know what to wear." Bentley had changed outfits four times this morning, finally settling on a light blue shirt, grey trousers, brogues, and a nice blazer. He sometimes didn't change his outfit four times in a week, let alone in one morning, but an overwhelming desire to impress gripped him and shook him with a violence that almost scared Bentley. Long gone were the days he'd wanted to impress someone, a feeling he'd missed.

"You look exactly as you should. Whether you are happy with your appearance right now or not does not matter, for all will change once the portrait is done." Miranda crossed the room and pulled a long curtain along the back wall, leaving only the light from the kitchen to illuminate the room.

"Don't artists like natural light?" Bentley asked, draining his coffee.

"I have good instincts, I don't need the light," she replied. "Place yourself on the stool or stand before it, either is fine."

Bentley did as he was told, seating himself on the chair and facing Miranda, though he couldn't see her as the easel blocked the way. Behind her was the kitchen, to the right the door. Either side the blank walls stretched endlessly, an infinite magnolia sea. Waves rippled along the walls, back and forth.

"Is this, is this okay?"

Foolishness flushed through him, an overwhelming urge to escape. Why did he think this was a good idea? A lurch in his stomach nearly threatened to escape up his throat. The beer gut he'd developed during a torrid twelve months, the wink of cold on the top of his balding head; laughter rang out, not from any one place, but all around, as if this empty room hosted a large crowd. The laughter was familiar, his ex-wife and her young lover, laughing, panting, moaning each other's names.

A voice cut through to Bentley.

"You're doing fine, Bentley, just focus."

Miranda's voice. Hers, and yet not. Like words travelling over a wall, from someone nearby and yet, by virtue of the wall, far away.

Coldness fired at Bentley's head and his hands flailed at the source, certain it was a flame or sharp implement. Pins entered his face at his sullen eyes, drooping cheeks, beneath his chin, needling away as if sewing him anew. A chainsaw sliced its serrated blades into his stomach, carving away sections deemed needless. Bentley held in the scream. Something told him to scream would be to give up, to

133

concede to this dark force, even as chunks of him sploshed on a floor coming to resemble a vulture's dream.

"Almost done!" Miranda cried.

Warm blood dripped down his legs, and Bentley leant back on the chair, struggling to remain upright. Each sharp implement retreated, replaced with stitching and the caress of brush strokes, reminding him of long-lost days with his wife, the loving touch of another.

The curtain rail squeaked as Miranda yanked the drapes across and the room flushed with natural light. Seconds later she held him, one arm on his back, another across his chest, and the pleasant smell of her breath warmed his cheek.

Bentley opened his eyes.

"You're okay," she said, smiling, "you can stand, it's over now. Please, go take a look in the mirror." Miranda's hands manoeuvred him upright and, to his shock, his legs worked fine. If anything, they felt stronger. A whiff of iron snuck up at him: the drip-sheets were thick with blood.

"Just go to the mirror, Bentley," Miranda whispered.

Dutifully, he did so.

Bentley's hands traversed the thick, robust hair of his head, his taut, chiselled face, muscular arms and chest, even his firm bottom. The person staring back was still him, but it also wasn't. Vibrant, handsome, youthful. In other words, a total stranger.

"Fuck," he said, holding the vowel. He swivelled, faced Miranda with wild eyes, held his hands out before his eyes like a beggar. "How?"

"There exists an irrevocable connection between you and I, something animalistic, base. Sexual, primal, something that demands attention. I feel protective of you. When this connection exists, I do my best work. Art is an expression of the subconscious, and I tap into your deepest desires. Do you feel… alive?" Miranda's azure eyes fixated on him, devoured every inch of the new Bentley. Her mouth hung open, tongue sliding across her top lip. She pressed herself against him, backed him against the wall, breath warming his neck, igniting long dormant senses.

"Can I see it? The painting?" he whispered, looking over Miranda's shoulder.

"No!" she gasped, clinging to him tight, kissing his neck, running her hands through his hair. "You cannot see it. Now come, follow me."

***

It had taken a while, but that was the last of the boxes emptied of clothes and trinkets. A single cardboard box of old framed photos and gifts called to him from its place by the door, begged him to reconsider his decision. But Bentley knew the time was right.

Standing over the box, he raised his left hand and slipped the gold band from his ring finger, dropped it in the box. A satisfying ding rang out as it bounced off an old jewellery box his ex-wife gifted him for his thirtieth birthday.

A lifetime ago.

Bentley carried the box down the stairs and out into the alley. A cat scarpered from behind a pile of wooden planks and shrapnel.

"I hear you, buddy," Bentley muttered.

The box crunched as it landed in the bin. Those memories smashed long ago.

Back upstairs, he walked around his apartment, cast an eye over the newly organised bookshelf, the toiletries neatly ordered in the bathroom, the freshly purchased pots and pans in his small kitchen, and nodded with satisfaction at the restoration of order to his world.

Something felt wrong, though he couldn't put a finger on it.

His mobile phone rested on the coffee table by the sofa. He thought about calling Miranda but remembered the old rule about waiting three days. It had been a long time since he'd dated.

The mirror demanded him once again and he stood before the mantelpiece—now home to an old, gold-faced clock of his grandfather's—looking at his rejuvenated features. The story of Narcissus sprung to mind, so he tore himself away, fearful of the pitfalls of vanity.

He picked up the phone.

***

Bentley glared at the phone, willed it to buzz, to ring, to vibrate, do something. But it lay there on the table next to his Styrofoam coffee cup, inert and, ironically, immobile. He grimaced at his little joke, unable to muster a fully-fledged smile. He'd left messages, sent texts, but Miranda hadn't replied. The elation he'd felt on that day in her apartment, the knowledge he'd been drawn to his physical peak, of near perfection, siphoned away with every passing second. If there was truth to the words Miranda uttered to him after his rebirth, probity in her whispered yearnings as they writhed beneath the sheets, then she'd contact him.

He grabbed the local newspaper from the pile on the side and flicked through it. Sure enough, the advert remained in its little lonely-hearts style, and that odd phrase, the one that ensnared him in the first place, screamed inside his head:

Do you want to see the perfect version of yourself?

Across the room, a woman's eyes risked a glance above her book. She lowered it, rouged lips offering a slip of a smile, both coy but inviting.

Bentley turned away and gazed out the café window, too weary to entertain another salacious stare. Down below, throngs of people milled back and forth holding shopping bags and pushing trolleys or prams, leaves whipping round there feet like thrashing piranha.

And there she was, a familiar face emerging from the piranha infested waters. Bentley knocked his chair over and fussed over righting it. He took the stairs two at a time and shoved through the glass door and out into the crowd. The cold breeze nipped at his cheeks. Their eyes met.

"Carol," Bentley said, stepping towards his ex-wife, "how've you been?"

"You look different," she said, surveying Bentley with a wary eye, "good, even."

"Just looking after myself. Going to the gym, moisturising, getting a good night's sleep."

Carol, in tight-fitting gym gear herself, raised an eyebrow and clucked her tongue. "All the things I asked you to do then. Interesting."

Bentley sighed and looked past Carol, noticed a young man in matching gym clothes eyeing her with impatience. "Puppy training going well, I see."

She looked over her shoulder, shook her head. "Same old bitter Bentley, I see. There's a reason we didn't work out and it's the same reason things will never work out for you," Carol said, turning back to him.

"Is it because you stole all my money?" he quipped, crossing his arms.

The cold breeze whipped up, muttered insults in Bentley's ear. He ruffled the hair around his ears, snatched at invisible mouths.

Carol huffed an impatient, cold white breath, and shook her head in disdain. The next four words she chose carefully, words she said with a deliberate malice. "You're nothing, Bentley, empty."

Before he could throw back a retort or laugh in her face or, or, just do anything, she was gone. Gone amongst the crowd, off with the young man who'd waited patiently for her. The taste and smell of iron filled Bentley's head. He'd bitten his bottom lip, split it open on the inside.

The woman who'd made eyes at him in the café passed, that smile long gone, only a steely dead-ahead look remaining.

Bentley spat a globule of blood at the ground and stormed off up the high street with only one destination in mind.

***

"Miranda! Miranda!"

Bentley pounded the door, drawing eyes from the hairdressers next door. He didn't care. They had a connection, and he couldn't ignore that or allow it to slip away.

A window opened above and a head of long, brunette hair appeared. "Bentley? What are you doing here?"

"Miranda! Let me up, please, we need to talk."

"About what, Bentley?"

He stumbled back, mouth hanging open.

Whether Miranda took pity on him or had a change of heart, he didn't know, but she told him to wait a moment and disappeared. A minute later the door opened, and he entered, followed her up to the studio apartment.

"Coffee?" she said in a casual way, as if Bentley hadn't half broken down the door and caused a scene in the street.

The room was exactly as he'd left it, but the portrait was covered with a dark cloth. The cloth's corners fluttered as if acted upon by an impossible wind. Something urged Bentley to raise the cover and see the elusive work, but Miranda's reaction when he'd asked the question suggested something dreadful.

Dreadful, but enticing.

"Coffee?" Miranda repeated, hands on hips. She wore a royal blue jumper and leggings, and flecks of red paint covered her front.

"No, no thank you. Why didn't you return my calls?" Bentley sounded like a wounded animal.

"Oh, I see. Bentley, I thought you knew what this was," she said, a coy chuckle spilling out.

"I thought we had a connection, something primal. We, we slept together!"

"A connection doesn't have to last, Bentley, it can be the beautiful ephemeral too. Listen, what we had was special, but you were just another subject, ultimately. Everything I committed to canvas, your transformation, it came from inside you. You're a beautiful shell, Bentley, a vision of perfection, enjoy it." Miranda walked around the kitchen counter, placed a hand beneath Bentley's chiselled chin, and cocked her head, a sympathetic smile twisting her face into something grotesque.

"You were supposed to show me perfection. Fuck. The painting," Bentley said, shoving her hand away.

"You can't! You won't be able to—"

Bentley pushed the protesting Miranda aside and took the corners of the cloth covering the portrait in both hands and yanked it off.

The image, in all its horrific glory, was beyond his comprehension. It snarled and undulated, slithered within the borders confining it to the realm of potential, its eternal prison. Bentley heard himself scream, felt himself hit the floor, scramble backwards until his back hit a wall. The long plain walls either side of the room stretched on into oblivion, the world where the image in the portrait existed. A wretched stench of flayed, mangled flesh filled the room.

Miranda rushed forward and flung the cover over the portrait again. This shut out the sensations assailing Bentley, left only a ringing in his ears and phantom pains all over his body, remnants of the agonies his physical form remembered well.

"You understand now what I took from you, Bentley. You can't go back," Miranda said, offering him her hand.

"What are you?" he asked, taking her hand.

"Just an artist, Bentley."

***

Bentley poured a whiskey and, wearing only a towel, collapsed onto his sofa. He could hear her in the shower. After leaving Miranda's, he'd gone drinking, imagining it the only way to fill the hole inside himself, picturing the hole spilling over with amber liquid. And, of course, the woman from the café had walked into the bar. He'd approached, charmed her with pithy remarks and wit, and brought her back to his apartment where they'd devoured each other in a desperate haze, like wolves tearing into a fresh kill.

He couldn't remember her name. Not that it mattered.

Bentley sipped whiskey and stared at the blank wall.

Ophelia in the Underworld

In the dim rouge light of the room, rose-scented candles glowed incandescent as the Valentine's Day ritual began. Four young couples stood in a circle, naked, save for the elaborate and detailed wolf masks they wore. They held hands and watched in silence as the candles within the circle flickered. Chairs, sofas, and a bed were pushed against the walls of the room.

Ophelia stepped forward, the waves of her deep red hair crashing around her lycanthrope mask. She lifted a violin to her naked shoulder, resting the cold wood in the nook, and began to play. Her body swayed sensually with the notes. She drew the bow back and forth with elegance and lightness, the speed increasing and then decreasing, the volume rising then falling. The music flowed like honey, its sweet scent rolling upon them and igniting their senses. An otherworldly emotion began to rise in each person. They became like coiled springs. Ophelia's playing had a musicality and lyricism that no other violinist in the world could hope to achieve. It was gift, a blessing, a miracle.

The circle continued to hold hands. Their grips tightened as the melody in turn gripped them. Their senses heightened as if the music was infecting them with some superpower or medicine. Chests heaved, inhalation and exhalation like the contours of a mountain range. A visible sexuality veiled the room, as though Ophelia's violin were releasing a pheromone-tinted scent.

The song came to an end. Ophelia placed her violin back in its case and strode into the centre of the circle.

"And now for the celebration of health and fertility," she declared, turning to her tall, dark-haired partner, running her hand over his cornrows, along his high cheekbones, and then down his chest. A second person set a record on a player and the doom-laden tones opening Wagner's Tristan and Isolde prelude started up. With this, the couples fell upon each other, kissing, caressing, in harmony with the orchestra. The four couples slowly writhed in unison, an ecstasy of humanity, a bonfire of necessity, longing. But not simply with their partners. They swapped, interchanged, man sleeping with man, woman sleeping with woman, black with white, white with black, brown with white, black with brown, over the course of a full, manic, ceremonial hour.

***

Ophelia stepped out into the cold city street, dimly lit, and linked arms with her partner, Charles. She was wearing a leather jacket, blue jumper, and skinny jeans, while Charles wore a grey winter overcoat, black knitted jumper, and jeans. Valentine's Day had ended as of a few minutes ago. Their small group held an annual celebration linked to Lupercalia, the ancient Roman festival with ties to the wolf and the foundation of Rome, to wish for health, fertility, and prosperity for the coming year. They sealed this with a gift of Earthly delights dedicated to the Old Gods.

Car horns honked in the distance. New York city. It never slept, was never quiet. Even in February and past midnight. The young couple rounded a corner in their downtown neighbourhood, which comprised apartment blocks, a central park but not *the* Central Park, grocery stores, liquor stores, a florist. A small, homely neighbourhood.

"I'm exhausted," Charles said, grinning widely and nudging Ophelia with his shoulder.

"So you should be," she responded, returning his smile and meeting those big brown eyes of his for just a second before turning away. "I love you," she added, almost as an afterthought.

Charles stopped them on the sidewalk by an alleyway and stepped in front of Ophelia, embracing her, kissing her, nestling his face into her hair, kissing her pale ear. "I love you too," he whispered.

Ophelia playfully pushed him away but couldn't stop herself giggling. "Yeah yeah, come on you, it's late. Oh shit," she said, looking herself up and down, "I forgot my violin."

"Oh Offy. No problem, run back and get it. I'll wait here," said Charles, leaning in to kiss Ophelia on the cheek, then nodding back in the direction they had come.

As Ophelia walked away, Charles watched her, his hand in his pocket, thumbing something with a nervousness he hadn't previously shown. He removed his hand from his pocket, his fingers clasped around a small, felt-covered object. A ring box. His grip on it tightened and he stared up at the moon and stars, shaking his head.

***

Ophelia waited for the apartment to buzz her up. Luckily, Carla hadn't settled down to sleep yet. After a quick exchange of pleasantries in the doorway, Carla passed Ophelia her violin case and she made the slow climb back downstairs.

"I'm never living higher than the third floor," said Ophelia to herself as she pushed through the door and stepped back out into the empty street. Wispy white breath instantly appeared before her. Ophelia allowed her heart rate to decrease after the staircase exertion, then set off walking. As she rounded the corner, she saw a cloaked figure running into the park, quickly lost among the trees and darkness.

Birds burst from the branches of trees in the middle of the park, disturbed by something. They caught Ophelia's eye and she followed them as they scattered. She noticed the lights still on in some apartments. People rowing, watching television, listening to music, having sex, talking, eating, drinking. Truly a city that never sleeps. She couldn't see Charles up ahead. The violin case felt unusually heavy. Ophelia reached the alleyway they had stopped beside. A convenient streetlamp meant she was bathed in light like an angelic apparition.

146

"Where has that boy got to?" she muttered as she glanced about.

Something else caught her eye. Right by her feet were glistening scarlet droplets, slowly seeping into the concrete paving, melding with the ever-present dirt. Ophelia, overcoming the stifling fear that had prevented her from doing so already, looked into the dark alleyway. Beyond the extended arm of the streetlamps glow, she could see the outline of something lay on the floor.

It was the unmistakable outline of a human being, and it was still.

Ophelia gasped. She ran to the figure and dropped to her knees. Her violin case slid off her shoulder and she pushed it aside. Even through denim the concrete was cold on her knees. Thick locks of hair fell beside her face as she leant over the prostrate, beautiful figure of Charles, and tears formed in her eyes.

Charles was lay on his back, his coat gone. Blood trailed from the corner of his mouth and a wide spherical bloodstain had spread through his jumper. Already the blood had pooled around him. An ethereal figure hovered above the scene and, to him, the blood was spreading into the shape of a heart.

Ophelia was knelt beside the lifeless body. She noticed something that had rolled aside. It was a ring box, open, empty, lying in a puddle and resembling a sinking ship. Ophelia let out a cry. She was crying out for lost love and a lost future symbolised by the empty and desolate ring box. She was crying out for the death of understanding and comfort and acknowledgement and back rubs and hot cocoa on cold evenings and forehead kisses and the strong warm embrace she couldn't imagine not experiencing every single day. Everything that Charles's death represented to her, not simply the loss of his life. An unconscious hand reached for her violin case, unclipped it, and pulled out the violin. Resting it in the nook of her neck and raising the bow, Ophelia played Charles's Lament. Tears fell as she evoked a sense of loss through music that reverberated across this world and the next. Doves flittered above the alley, materialising as if from the ether. The birds flew around the floating figure of Mephistopheles. Unable to contain himself further, he drifted down to rest beside the lonely Ophelia. She continued to play.

"There is a way to save him," Mephistopheles said, his blazing red eyes gazing down upon the lovers, one dead, one alive. Flaming tears draped his cheeks before dropping to the ground.

The demon was in human form, save for his feathered black wings and red eyes. But though his form was human, there was something unhuman about it. Skin paler than Death's horse, hair blacker than night, tousled and held in a stylised form that should not have been possible. His body sculpted like the figures in a renaissance painting, idealised yet impossible. He was naked, having no need for clothing. As a demon, he ran hot.

Ophelia stopped playing. She looked up but didn't react. She couldn't react, for her eyes could not fully comprehend the vision before her and its strange yet morbid beauty.

"Your song is beyond anything that should be possible in this world," Mephistopheles said. The demon leant forward and placed a hand on Ophelia's shoulder. It was a warm hand. "You can save him, but it is task that requires heroism and the blessing of the Gods."

"What is it? Tell me what it is and I will do it. Anything for him," Ophelia said, placing her violin back in its case. She looked up at the doves now circling above. Their startling whiteness appeared like stars or snowdrops against the night sky.

"You will need that instrument, Ophelia. It will be your only weapon in the battle to come. Already, your lover's soul will have made its journey to the Underworld, ruled by Hades, populated by Death. I can open a portal for you to get there, but you must reach Hades and convince him to return your lover's departed soul to its body. It was by chance I overheard your song and it so enraptured me, tormented me, tortured me like a rhapsody from the lyre of Apollo himself. I could not fail to stop and offer my help. So will you accept my offer? Will you travel to the Underworld to try to save this man's soul?" Mephistopheles said. He stood up to his full height and held his arms out, palms facing up.

Ophelia nodded. "Yes, I will."

"Remember when you arrive to travel by the means you would expect to travel," Mephistopheles said, proffering a hopeful smile.

Ophelia picked her violin up and the bow and watched Mephistopheles. A bright red light formed in his hands and he drew a door in the air, a fizzling, floating outline, an entrance to a realm that was other, a realm known as the Underworld.

Without a word, Mephistopheles gestured towards the doorway. Ophelia, clutching her violin, closed her eyes and walked through.

***

Ophelia opened her eyes expecting what one should expect when entering the Underworld. Gates of fire, Hell Hounds, murky rivers with lone ferrymen, the screams of tortured souls, phantoms and devils racing about, myriad Hellish things. Instead, what Ophelia saw was…

"Starbucks? Is this… Hell?"

Rising all around Ophelia was a modern metropolis not unlike Manhattan, with skyscrapers of glass and brick and grey and silver like medieval swords thrust into the ground or rising like the hands of the living dead pushing up through the dirt beneath which they were buried, depending on your perspective. Either way, it was a dead city, inert, empty. And that was the crucial detail that chilled Ophelia's blood; there wasn't a soul in sight. Stepping out into the street, she looked up and down the seemingly endless thoroughfare and saw nothing. A barren landscape when by rights it should be the loudest and liveliest of places.

Ophelia clutched her violin and bow tight to her chest. Not knowing what to do or where to go, she turned back to the Starbucks and entered.

It was quiet. No music was playing, and the familiar sounds of coffee machines and chatter were conspicuous by their absence, like a concert hall without an audience or orchestra. Empty tables sat to the right and left and straight ahead was the path to the counter, flanked by cold fridges full of soft drinks and sandwiches.

"Does anyone work here?" said Ophelia, edging forwards.

"There is time not for dalliances with us lowly spectres," a voice called through from the backroom behind the counter.

Ophelia strode forward and found herself face to face with a translucent being, what was formerly a man, of that she was sure, but now just a... ghost? A phantom? Wearing a Starbucks apron? The nametag read, 'Jim'.

"Tell me where to go, Jim," said Ophelia, the bow in her right hand assuming a dual usage as she pointed it with menace at the faded human form before her. A middle-aged man, Jim was balding and had blue watery eyes. Though this was difficult to discern as there was also something utterly... grey about him. Ophelia found it difficult to focus.

"Look lady, are you going to order or what?" Jim said impatiently, looking over her shoulder.

Inhaling deeply, Ophelia span round and gasped; there was a queue of spirits and sprites and spectres and demons waiting, glaring angrily at the reason for the hold-up. It felt hot, heat rising through her feet as if she were walking on hot coals. The demon stood directly behind her leant forward and tapped her on the shoulder, pointing toward the menu on the board. Its face was snake-like, with yellow eyes and slits for a nose. The finger was long and elongated like it had five or six joints. A forked tongue flickered from the corner of its smirking mouth. Ophelia fell back into the counter.

"Lady?!"

Ophelia turned to find Jim's translucent form was now vibrant and firm, his face full of the redness of roses.

"A coffee, please, just a coffee"

"Christ, what type? We've got a lot."

"You choose, dammit," Ophelia replied. Silence fell upon the café and Jim's colour faded. Ophelia had screamed her response to Jim with the force of a shotgun blast and Jim was reeling as if it were a direct hit.

"Sure thing, lady, sure thing," he said, busying himself. "Name?" he added, glancing over his shoulder.

"Ophelia."

"Got it. Please move along to the end counter, your drink will be with you shortly," Jim said, scrawling in black ink on the Styrofoam cup and passing it to a colleague who had materialised out of nowhere.

Ophelia moved down the row. The snake-like demon behind her cast a look her way that suggested he was afraid. He walked in such a way as to keep his physical form as far from Ophelia as were possible in such a confined space.

Slowly, noise returned to the Starbucks and Ophelia, leaning against the end of the counter, examined the array of faces. They were black, brown, white, but then there was green, blue, red, yellow, and other hues in between. There were alligator jaws and wings and fangs and claws that did not ordinarily frequent Starbucks coffee shops. And a smell on the air of coffee and… dirt? Earth? Ophelia could not place it.

"Here you go," said an unfamiliar voice, placing a cup of coffee on the counter.

"Thanks," Ophelia said, absently picking up her drink. She raised it to her face and noticed the name scrawled on it: 'Offy'.

"Hey, why did you write this?" Ophelia cried, taking in the familiar shape of the letters, the elegant and ostentatious curvature of the ff that marked this handwriting out as belonging to Charles.

There was no answer to her cry.

Looking up, Ophelia saw the building was empty. Silence drowned her once more.

***

Ophelia let the door swing shut behind her and stepped back out into the street. She continued to stare at the letters etched in black ink on the cup. No one called her Offy, no one, not her mother or her sister, not her father or her grandfather. But Charles did. It was his pet name for her.

"What kind of twisted game is this?" she muttered.

Surrounded by towering buildings, Ophelia collapsed onto the kerb and sat there drinking her coffee. It tasted bitter. That bitterness took her far away, deep into a recurring memory, a memory of Saturday mornings spent practicing the violin at the rooms her orchestra rented for such purposes. The memory ended the exact same way each time; Charles poking his head around the door, a wide smile on his face and two coffees in hand. A bag of bagels tucked neatly under his arm. It was a memory she loved because of its dual warmth: the warmth of Charles's love for her and the warmth of the hot drink on cold winter mornings when she needed it most. Charles didn't need to do that. He could have stayed in their apartment and slept in or done anything else for that matter. Instead, without fail, he'd traipse uptown to the practice studios to meet her. They had made love right there in the room, once or twice. Only after Charles had been away for work during the week and they'd seen less of each other. But, always, they longed for each other in these absences and made up for lost time at the first opportunity.

Ophelia wiped a tear from her eye. The kerb felt cold beneath her. She felt... empty. Looking left and right, along the vacant thoroughfare, she felt this emptiness tenfold. Like a hollowed-out tree with nothing left to do but rot and die.

On the verge of slipping into a well of despair, Ophelia did her best to breathe deeply and focus her mind. She drank some coffee. She placed her head on her knees and she concentrated.

Where had the people and the creatures come from and where had they gone? Ophelia shook her head and drank some more. Her violin sat on the ground beside her. The claws of despair tightened their grip. Until something occurred to her, some odd kernel that had bothered Ophelia the moment she'd heard it.

"What did he say? 'Travel by the means you'd expect to travel', wasn't it? Well, this looks like New York city," Ophelia said. Drinking the remains of her coffee, she threw it into a nearby bin, retrieved her violin, stood by the kerb, and held out a hand, thumb up.

And then the sound of car horns filled the air. A blare as loud as a football game. Though no cars appeared before her the noise was deafening and a sense of being surrounded threatened to drown Ophelia. The emptiness she had felt was suddenly filled too quickly and teetered on the edge of spilling over. Filling that

155

emptiness was anxiety, dread. The car horns were like the screams of the dead and Ophelia remembered where she was: the Underworld.

In the distance, a yellow speck grew larger. Gradually, the full outline of a yellow New York style taxi cab hurtled into view. Pulling up before Ophelia, who'd jumped back in response, its tyres screeched like fighting alley-cats.

The window wound down.

"Where to, young lady?" said a voice with the most New York of New York accents. Ophelia bent down to look through the open window. A middle-aged man with olive skin, a salt-and-pepper moustache, wearing a frayed flat cap, was smiling at her.

"Take me to Hades, please," Ophelia said, not moving from the sidewalk.

The driver looked puzzled. "You want to see the boss man? You're talking crazy, why would you wanna do that?"

"I have to see him, I'm looking for someone I love," Ophelia's hands were on the door, her face almost in the car.

"Ohhhh, I see. Well, you got your silver coin? It's one silver coin for the trip. Honestly, it's pretty unusual you're already here because I normally meet people right on the edge of town by the bridge…" he said, giving her a curious up-and-down look, as if coming to a slow realisation. "Hey, you aren't dead, are you? Crazy. Well, good luck to you, but I can't help. No payment, no passage… I mean trip. Still used to using the old language, you know? This place has changed a lot. Don't know if I'm coming or going if I'm honest with you. Modernisation, eh? I prefer the old ways..." the driver said, turning to face forward and put the car in drive.

"Wait," Ophelia cried, her head still hanging through the window. "What if I play something for you? I have my violin." With this, she flung herself backwards and retrieved her instrument.

"Well, it's highly irregular... but okay. It has the feel of the old ways, you know? You play something to buy passage, I like that. Used to put old Cerberus to sleep, a bit of music. She works in accounts now. Waste of a good three-headed dog if you ask me... but anyway, go ahead," the driver said, putting the car back in park.

As if in expectation, the city noises and car horns and engines abruptly went silent. The hush of an expectant audience fell over the city street and Ophelia, comfortable in such an atmosphere, relaxed.

Placing the violin in the nook of her neck, Ophelia exhaled, in the same manner a sniper might before taking a shot, then began to play.

Watching Ophelia play, the driver's eyes stared unblinking at her, a slow intoxication taking place. Quietly, he opened the driver's side door and stepped out of the car and leant his arms and head on top of it. The music took him back to a time when he understood his place in the world, to a place that felt more like home, more comfortable. And then it took him further back, to childhood, to stories of the

157

Gods and heroes and tremendous monsters and epic tales. Removing his flat cap, he held it to his chest and wept. Stood in this metropolis of modern monsters. Skyscrapers looming like sentries. Endless days. Meaningless, repetitive. Charon smiled through his tears and asked Ophelia to stop. Walking round the taxi cab, he opened the door and gestured for her to enter.

***

Charon drove for a good while and Ophelia leant her head against the window, feeling the vibrato of the car against her skin. At each turn, she expected something new or different, but it never came. There was something labyrinthine about the city and its emptiness exacerbated its labyrinthine nature. Ophelia would worry how to make it out later.

Abruptly, the taxi screeched to a halt. Charon evidently didn't care much for his brakes.

"Good luck, young lady. You keep tight hold of that violin, you'll need it," he said, raising a hand in goodbye.

Ophelia climbed out and the taxi cab promptly drove off, soon out of sight. She turned to look at the building Charon had dropped her off outside. Marble blocks flanked a short path leading to the glass entrance and within each block was a small olive tree bedded into a compost pile. Gold trimmed the window frames of the building and they glittered despite the grey, dull, sunless sky above. The tower was, otherwise, exactly the same grey glassy metallic monstrosity that was a feature of the Underworld. Ophelia felt the cold again and shivered.

She walked up toward the entrance, violin and bow in hand. She pushed through the all-glass revolving door and walked along the white marble floor. A reception desk complete with receptionist was before her and behind them was an elevator. The silence was disturbed by the mechanical sound of an elevator descending. It stopped on the ground floor and a pleasant ding indicated the door was about to open.

A woman stepped out. A ghostly woman with brunette hair reaching down her back, she wore a flowing white dress that was completely at odds with her surroundings. Her head was garlanded with a wreath of white flowers. As she approached Ophelia, she saw there was an ethereal beauty to her features. Ophelia could hardly hold eye contact with the woman but knew she must. She felt almost as if the woman were challenging her and it was crucial she rise to it. The woman smiled.

"I understand Mephistopheles sent you." It was not a question, so Ophelia maintained her gaze and stayed quiet. "He is a demon after my own heart for he appreciates beauty and the arts, something sorely lacking in my... husband. I am Persephone. I am sure by now you understand that everything you are experiencing is real. Perhaps you should know that everything you thought of as myth, and yes, even those you perform offerings to each Valentine's Day, are real. What you are about to do is real and the risk is all too real. Before you speak with my husband and make your case, I want you to acknowledge you understand what I have told you. I know all too well the trickery of the Gods."

Persephone placed her left hand on Ophelia's shoulder and gently massaged the nook in which her violin would sit.

"If you should fail, you will have lost Charles forever. Worse still, my husband has a malevolent side. He is fiendish. He enjoys punishing people when they do not live up to his expectations. And he does so… creatively. If you wish to continue, please follow me."

Ophelia stared into the doleful brown eyes of Persephone and sensed she was pleading with her to turn back. But she had come too far. Charles needed her to save him just as she needed to save Charles.

"I'm ready," Ophelia said.

***

The elevator journey was short, complete with typical elevator music. Ophelia found it strange that this detail had been included in the rendering of the modern city, but when she remembered she was in Hell, it suddenly made sense.

The doors opened up into an expansive, elegant office with a 360 degree view of the cityscape below them. For this was the tallest building in a city of giants. Sofas sat either side of a ruby red rug that ran the length of the space between the elevator door and the solid oak desk. Behind that desk sat a man in a leather-backed black chair. His black hair was slicked back, raven-esque, and his facial hair trimmed into a perfect black goatee. He rose from his seat and walked around the desk. His suit was tailored, black with white pinstripes, and his white shirt cuffs were held in place with silver cufflinks that shone in the strangely unnatural light of the office.

"Ophelia, my dear, how nice of you to come and see me. It's been a long time since anyone made the journey. And I do so adore music, though not as much as Persephone, which I'm sure she's already mentioned. And here you are with your violin and holding it like it's loaded with live rounds. Please understand I'm not the big bad you may believe, I'm just the unlucky custodian of the Underworld. And there are rules for the Underworld," the man added, shrugging his shoulders.

"I was sent here by Mephistopheles in order to see Hades. I assume you are Hades?" Ophelia asked, realising the man had not introduced himself. She felt a strong urge to take control of the conversation or at least knock him from his stride. Clearly, Hades was a loquacious God.

"Where are my manners? But of course, I am Hades, Lord of the Underworld," he said, bowing low, almost mockingly.

"I've come to ask you return Charles to life. He doesn't deserve to die!" said Ophelia. She realised that now she was here, she had no rhetoric prepared, no idea how she was to argue for her lover's soul. She was not, as she had recently declared, 'ready'.

"I'm afraid death is somewhat arbitrary, Ophelia. There are those who deserve to die and do not, and those who do not deserve to die and yet they do. While it is indeed impressive that you so caught the attention of Mephistopheles that he opened a portal to the Underworld for you, and that you have found your way here, catching a free ride from Charon, I might add, we ultimately land upon me. And I remain unconvinced as to why I should return Charles to life. I note you attended a festival of sorts this evening, one in which you each engaged in sexual relations not just with each other but with several different men and women. Forgive me, but is it not traditional Valentine's fare—in modernity, at least—to express your romantic love to an individual solely, and not to a group? If I am to bend the rules for someone, I need a good reason. Can you provide me with one?" Hades asked, strolling around his office and gazing out of the windows.

"We engage in a festival with a small group of friends on Valentine's Day each year to celebrate and wish for good health and good prospects for the coming year. It's linked to the ancient festival of..."

"Lupercalia, yes," interjected Hades, circling Ophelia, as if sizing her up. "A tenuous link and an odd justification for such behaviour. How can you feel so strongly for one individual yet engage in relations with others?"

"Ask Zeus," Persephone muttered, now lounging on a chaise longue and looking every inch the mythological figure and inspiration for renaissance artworks.

"Well, quite. But my point remains," Hades said.

"Because the connection Charles and I share is stronger than that. No, we don't fit the standard couple archetype, we do enjoy sex with other people, and this does include our little get together every Valentine's Day. Our trust and relationship foregoes the jealousies that might destroy others. For us, sharing our bodies heightens the pleasure and variety of our sex life, which in turn strengthens our bond. This might not be the norm, but it's something that works for us. Yes, the connection to Lupercalia is tenuous but we're somewhat spiritual without having any fixed ideas or strict dogma. We believe powers beyond ourselves exist—and from what Persephone has told me, it seems most of them *do* exist—so we honour them and give thanks with an annual expression of joy. Yes, we've just picked up on something, mutated it, and run with it. But our little festival, little ritual each year, has taken on a significance to us beyond its spurious beginnings.

"Charles and I are rare in that we fully understand everything about each other and, not only do we accept every little thing, we like them too. We are perfect for each other and my existence will forever be broken without him. Please, I'm here to beg you if necessary, return him to me. I know you spend time apart from Persephone each year, assuming the stories are true. But at least for half the year she returns to you. If Charles dies, I do not have that luxury."

163

Ophelia let out a sigh and sagged. She couldn't remember the last time she had said so many words uninterrupted, like a Shakespearean soliloquy. And there were people who talked this much for a living, something for which she had a newfound level of respect.

"You make an… interesting case," Hades said, joining Persephone on the chaise longue. He ran his hand along her luminous cheek and she nuzzled him in return. A smile touched the corners of Hades's mouth.

"Listen to her play, darling," said Persephone, her languid form failing to betray a significant interest in the events unfolding before her. Her eyes, however, were fixed upon her husband, perhaps looking for tell-tale signs of his mood and thoughts.

"You are right, of course, my dear. Ophelia, ultimately, you have come here not to bargain or beg for your lover's life, but to play for it. If music be the food of love, and so forth. Please, begin."

Ophelia raised her violin to sit in its favoured nook and cast one final glance at her rapt audience. Playing for a God was something new. She had played to people who thought they were gods for as long as she could remember. But an actual God? Well, if it weren't for trauma-tinged thoughts of Charles and the high stakes of the situation, she might have enjoyed this moment.

Raising the bow, she began.

Golden notes twisted lovingly. But then the tone of the music changed. Bitter and jagged, like waves crashing against a rocky coast, Ophelia's violin told a story of love and loss as if it were paint on a canvas, so clear was the narrative, so evocative was her playing. Persephone sat up straight and slipped her hand into Hades's. They were perched on the edge of the chaise longue and watching this young woman play just as forsaken sailors were drawn to the call of the Sirens. Hades squeezed Persephone's hand. Glancing at her husband, she saw the upturned corner of his mouth, a smirk that betrayed his natural malevolence.

Ophelia finished playing and her captive audience rose and applauded. In return she bowed, as was customary after a performance, no matter how unconventional the setting. A stifling silence filled the room without the sound of Ophelia's playing. Being a city girl, silence unsettled her.

Hades rose and moved towards the elevator. He gestured for Ophelia to follow. Hades pressed the button and waited for the lift to arrive, which it duly did and opened with a ding. He stepped in and turned. Ophelia did the same. As the doors closed, she caught once last look at Persephone, and saw glistening pearls tumbling down her face.

Walking through reception, Hades requested the receptionist call for Charon. They were now stood outside in the street, past the little olive trees in the marble blocks. It smelled of asphalt and exhaust fumes, just like any other city. Hades had said nothing to Ophelia as to his intentions. The street was as empty and quiet as it had been when Ophelia arrived. And windless, a forgotten aspect of this manufactured metropolis, the single missing element of realism.

Hades and Ophelia stood facing each other.

"I will have Charon transport you to the bridge over the River Styx, at which point you will reach the portal to take you home. As you walk across this bridge, Charles will follow you. However, there is a condition. You must not look back at Charles, you must not lay eyes on him, until you are both across the threshold of the bridge. Once you reach the other side, you will be safe to proceed. But you understand, if you look back at Charles, there will be consequences? These are the conditions I have set. Do you accept them?" Hades said, his hands clasped behind his straight back. In the light, in his suit, he resembled a shark.

A car engine could be heard in the distance.

Ophelia nodded a yes. She would have spoken but her entire system seemed not to be working properly, such was the exhilaration she felt when Hades spoke. Charles would not die. She was getting him back and they would be together. She would not lose him. They would be married. Her brain was a frenzy of similar such phrases flashing by at different volumes, in different colours, at different speeds. Walk across the bridge and don't look back. Simple. She could do that.

A yellow New York style taxi screeched to a halt beside them and Charon, window wound down, shouted to Ophelia as if they were long lost friends.

Without anything more being said, Ophelia, still clutching her violin and bow, clambered into the back of the car, and it quickly turned in the bare street and set off. Looking over her shoulder, she watched the suited figure of Hades, God of the Underworld, wave her off like a grandparent after a weekend stay.

"You did it, then?" enquired Charon, adjusting his flat cap with one hand while swinging the steering wheel with the other. Ophelia imagined it didn't require too much attention to drive along roads with no other drivers.

"I did. Hades heard me out and then listened to me play and he agreed to let Charles live. I just have to walk across the bridge without looking back at Charles and then we can go back to our lives."

In her joyous mood, Ophelia failed to spot the faltering smile of Charon. If she had glanced up at the rear-view mirror as she spoke, she would have seen his wide grin diminish ever-so-slightly, the difference being as subtle as the difference between burgundy and maroon or teal and turquoise. The colour in Charon's face faded. The remainder of the journey was quiet.

They soon emerged from the towering buildings and pulled up facing a suspension bridge. The sky above was grey, but a distinct change occurred just beyond the bridge, where it became a watery blue and white. Ophelia got out of the car and walked towards the bridge.

"Thank you, Charon," she said, turning and smiling and laughing, as if she had been on a great adventure.

Stood by his taxi cab, leaning on its roof, he nodded and raised his cap.

Ophelia took her first step onto the bridge and held her breath, stopping. Instantly, she could feel a presence behind her. She could hear breathing. She began walking again and could hear the faintest of footsteps following her, almost in unison. Ophelia's heart was beating harder than it ever had before and she trained her focus on the peculiar blueish sky ahead, realising now it was much harder than she had expected to not turn around to see Charles. To see her tall, dark, handsome lover, to tell him she loved him, to kiss him, touch him, smell him, all the things that occasionally embarrassed her in the real world. But she remained firm and walked forwards, her grip on her violin and bow tighter than usual, for fear she would drop them and lose her concentration.

Beyond the bridge was a watercolour of a forest, separating this world and the next as a vague, wall-like structure, the atmosphere of which resembled a waterfall. This was no doubt the portal they would have to cross to reach their home world again. The River Styx flowed below them and sounded treacherous to Ophelia. And then the cries began. Tortured, pained screams. Screams for help, for justice, for death. Ophelia stopped walking. The voices were coming from below. The flowing water was comprised of millions of souls and their eternal cries were the music Hades truly loved.

"Don't look back. Don't look back. Don't look back," Ophelia whispered to herself, continuing her crossing.

"Nearly there," she said, picking up her pace.

Ahead of her, passing through the translucent veil that was the portal, was Mephistopheles. A smile graced his beautiful face.

Ophelia started to run and, quickly reaching the other side, crossed the threshold. She carefully placed her violin and bow down on the ground, still facing forwards. As she did so, an anguished wail like nothing she had heard before assailed her senses. Though the voice had mutated, it was unmistakeably Charles. He could be in a crowd of thousands, all chanting, and Ophelia would recognise and pick out his voice.

Ophelia placed her hands against her ears, but the Hellish crescendo was impossible to block out. Was Charles being tortured? Was he being prevented from reaching her? And then a single word, discernible within the wall of noise.

"Offy!"

Ophelia could take no more.

She turned.

A call of 'no' could be heard but, mixed in with the din of eternal damnation flowing beneath the bridge and the abject, pitiable cries of Charles, Ophelia failed to identify the call or take heed.

Her eyes fixed on Charles's for a split second and then he was gone, his form dissipating into a billion tiny pieces. In the form of rain, they fell towards the river below.

"What's happening? Charles? No, no, no, Hades said!" cried Ophelia, doubling over in pain, hugging herself. She turned to Mephistopheles, his magnificent form reaching for her, tears streaking his face.

"You were to wait until you *both* crossed the threshold, Ophelia. Hades made one last attempt to trick you into turning" he said, embracing her, his dark wings folding around them. Within his grip she remained, crying, screaming, shouting into his chest. The demon held her for as long as it was needed, until, finally, he said it was time to leave.

***

It had been four years since Ophelia had travelled to the Underworld to try to save Charles's soul. Her failure tore at her daily. Some days were harder than others. For a long time, she had seen Charles's face everywhere. In crowded streets, on packed buses and trains, in her own reflection, even. These were the normal manifestations of grief. Back in the real world, the culprit was never found, but Ophelia didn't feel anything when it came to people asking for 'justice' for Charles. Her experience in the Underworld had drained her of any regular feelings towards his death.

Valentine's Day was, of course, the hardest time for Ophelia. It was not until the first anniversary of Charles's death that Ophelia realised the full extent of Hades's twisted sense of humour. But it should be no surprise that a God with a twisted sense of love should have a twisted sense of humour, and so it had unfolded as such. Sat in her apartment, staring out of a rain covered window, listening to the drops, she had seen a reflection in the glass. Turning, she was confronted by Charles standing over her. An initial elation had run through Ophelia, who had leapt up and attempted to embrace Charles. But she had passed right through him. This shade of Charles that appeared each year on Valentine's Day could not speak to her, could not touch her, could not kiss or hold her. But it appeared every year without fail, a tiny taste of what she could have had, had she only listened properly to Hades's instructions, not rushed ahead of herself, not fallen for his trickery.

But Ophelia refused to be driven mad by this shade of Charles that would not leave her side each year. She would not drown in her sorrows, as haunted as she was by his loss. It would mark her for the rest of her life, but Ophelia did not want to become some pitiable, lost soul. So after that first year she returned to their festival, to partake several lovers during the ritualistic euphoria the group engaged in as if nothing had changed. And, though the others were ignorant, she knew Charles was there. It was a twisted love affair she conducted with her memories of Charles and this shade of his soul that appeared annually.

Mephistopheles checked in on Ophelia intermittently, though never showing himself to her. He would watch these Valentine's Day shows and weep, knowing that in truth these violent delights would, in time, drive Ophelia to madness. And in

madness, Hades awaits.

Stephen Howard (he/him) is an English novelist and short story writer from Manchester, now living in Cheshire with his wife, Rachel, and their daughter, Flo. An English Literature and Creative Writing graduate from the Open University, his work has been published by Lost Boys Press, The No Sleep Podcast, and Dark Recesses Press, among others. He's also published one novel, a comic fantasy titled Beyond Misty Mountain, and the multi-genre short story collection titled Condemned To Be. Find Stephen at:

Twitter: @SteJHoward

Website: www.stephenhowardblog.wordpress.com

Printed in Great Britain
by Amazon

39384637R00097